KLAWDE

EVIL ALIEN WARLORD CAT

ENEMIES

BY JOHNNY MARCIANO
AND EMILY CHENOWETH

KLAWDE

EVIL ALIEN WARLORD CAT

ILLUSTRATED BY
ROBB
MOMMAERTS

ENEMIES

PENGUIN WORKSHOP

My name is Raj. I'm a regular kid from Brooklyn who just moved across the country to Elba, Oregon. I hated it when I was forced to come here, but now I kind of like it. I have a mom, a dad, and a very special cat—Klawde!

RAJ

KLAWDE

My name is not Klawde. It is Lord High Emperor Wyss-Kuzz, the Magnificent. I was exiled across the universe to this backward planet of furless ogres known as Earth. I hated it when I was forced to come here, and now I hate it even more.

CHAPTER 1

I was getting dressed *verrrrry* slowly. The reason: Today was the first day of middle school. This was scary enough for any kid, but I was living in a brand-new town, and that made it ten times worse.

I wished I could just crawl back under the covers, but Klawde was lying on my bed. He wasn't very nice about sharing, and I had the scratch marks to prove it.

"Do you think I'll know anyone?" I asked him. "I mean, besides Cedar and Steve and the kids from Camp Eclipse?" Unfortunately, those kids included Newt, who was always trying to mess with me, and Scorpion, who always picked on me. "I just hope there'll be other new kids in sixth grade."

If Klawde had an opinion about the matter, he didn't express it. He stretched and yawned in the little square of sunlight falling on the bed.

"The first time I see Newt, she'll probably try to trip me in the hallway," I said. "And Scorpion will step on my face."

Klawde swished his tail and rolled over.

What was the point of having a talking cat if he didn't actually *talk*? I loved him, but sometimes he could be pretty frustrating.

"Look at my schedule," I said, holding up the paper I'd printed out last night. It was so complicated, I needed to go to school just to be able to understand it.

"I've never had homeroom before," I said. "Or had to walk around a huge school all by myself. How will I find my classes? And Room 3.5—what does that even mean?"

"Raj! You're going to be late!" my mom called from downstairs.

I shoved some color-coded folders into my backpack, along with the rest of my new school supplies.

"Lunch isn't until next-to-last period. I'm gonna starve," I said. "And what kind of a class is 'RBX'? That's not even a word!"

Klawde opened his mouth, like he was finally about to say something. But he just yawned again. He rolled onto his back and let the sunlight fall on his furry belly.

	MONDAY	TUESDAY
PERIOD 1:	Homeroom Rm: 218	Homeroom Rm: 218
PERIOD 2:	Math Rm: 557C	Lunch Cafeteria
PERIOD 3:	Science Rm: Tbd	Gym S. Campus
PERIOD 4:	English Rm: 3.5	Math Rm: 557C
PERIOD 5:	Social Studies Rm: T	Science Rm: Tbd
PERIOD 6:	Gym S. Campus	English Rm: 3.5
PERIOD 7:	Lunch Cafeteria	RBX Rm: Lab RB
PERIOD 8:	RBX Rm: Lab RBX	Social Stud Rm: T

"Don't you have *anything* to say?" I asked him.

Klawde stretched all the way out and wriggled his toes.

"Oh, have you been speaking?" he said. "I wasn't paying attention."

CHAPTER 2

I was in a mood most foul.

My plans to *re*-reconquer my home planet were at a standstill, and it was all thanks to that cross-eyed fool, Flooffee-Fyr. Not only had my former lackey overthrown and exiled me, he had also closed all wormholes between Earth and Lyttyrboks, making a return presently impossible.

Luckily I knew that double-crossing nincompoop better than he knew himself. Flooffee could manage a coup, but *not* an entire planet of cats. I had been following the chaos on the Intra-Universal Feline News Feed. Any day now he would call me and *beg* for me to come back. And once I ruled Lyttyrboks for the third time, I would never again allow that power to slip through my claws!

In the meantime, however, I could do little but sit on my backside and watch the intergalactic cat phone, waiting for it to ring. I was so disturbed by this state of inaction that I had napped only eleven times yesterday. And now, when I was trying to catch up on my rest, the Human would not cease his inane blathering.

Though I pointedly ignored him, the boy-Human droned on about this new school of his. He was—as usual—helpless in the face of a challenge, and he begged me to share some of my wisdom with him.

Yawning, I took pity, and asked what they taught there.

"Poison Chemistry? Battle Tactics? The Art of Slash-and-Claw?"

He *would* be more useful once he had learned such basics.

But the Human informed me that he would be learning none of these essential skills.

"Haven't you been listening to *anything* I've said?"

I already told him I had NOT.

I inspected his diagram of classes. "A course in English?" I said, swishing my tail scornfully. "But that is a language you already speak! And lunch? You know how to eat!"

Although it *was* disgusting to watch.

"Where is Revenge 101?" I demanded. "Where is the Art of Ambush?"

Ah, the Art of Ambush! I remembered fondly how I had taught it to my most brilliant student—Ffangg.

That traitorous wretch.

The boy was still blathering, but thankfully the master of the house—the mother-Human—called up the stairs again.

"Raj, your friends Cedar and Steve are here!" she said. "You have to GO!"

"Wish me luck," he said.

I scoffed. "True warriors make their own luck!"

But I pitied him as he rushed away to this "middle school." Leave it to the hairless ogres, in their stupidity and shortsightedness, to create schools that taught nothing of importance.

That's when it hit me—my latest BRILLIANT idea!

The Humans may not teach the Art of Ambush, but *I* could. What if I set up a school? A school of my own.

A school for . . . **warriors**!

Purrrrr.

CHAPTER 3

On the walk to school, Cedar, Steve, and I took out our schedules, and as we compared them, I got a sinking feeling in my stomach.

We had almost *no* classes together.

"But we're in the same math class," Cedar said to me as we hung around the flag in front of the school, waiting for the doors to open. "And sometimes we have lunch together. And look—we all have Lab RBX!"

"Whatever *that* is," Steve said.

Bzzzzzzzzzzzzzzzzzzzzzzz!

At the sound of the bell, we hurried inside. A big monitor hung from the ceiling of the main hall and flashed a message in bright red letters:

WELCOME BACK, FIGHTIN' BOOKWORMS!

Was the school mascot really an earthworm

14

wearing boxing gloves? Worms didn't even *have* arms.

The first good news of the day was that I found my homeroom, no problem. (It was right inside the front door.) I sat down just before the tardy bell rang. When I looked around, I saw a bunch of kids I didn't know—but no teacher.

Suddenly, there was a booming voice, and I half jumped out of my seat.

"Hi, y'all! And welcome to your FIRST day at Elba Middle School!"

The voice was coming from a pair of speakers.

"Y'all can call me Miss Emmy Jo, and I'm your homeroom teacher."

Miss Emmy Jo had big glasses, orange hair, and a sweater with a glittering, sequined pony on it. She was *also* just a face on a smartboard screen.

"Now, y'all may think it's weird to have a teacher on a screen, but it's part of a new wave in education,"

Miss Emmy Jo said.

"Remote instruction!"

"Cool!" the kid behind me whispered. "We can do whatever we want!"

Miss Emmy Jo's bright blue eyes grew suddenly dark.

"No, you can *not* do whatever you want, Mr. Student Number Seventeen," she said. "I may be sitting down here in Alabama, but I can spy you like a vulture spies a wounded field mouse!"

All the students suddenly got *very* quiet.

"I have a split-screen monitor right here with every student's face on it," Miss Emmy Jo said. "My hushed-voice recognition technology not only detects whispers at twenty decibels, but also *who* is making them!"

Miss Emmy Jo's expression again suddenly switched, this time from a frown back into a big smile.

"I know we're gonna have the best homeroom year ever! Go Fightin' Mealworms!"

"Fightin' *Bookworms*!" someone in the back yelled.

Miss Emmy Jo looked down at her notes. "Right," she said. "Sorry about that, y'all! Skedaddle now, and have yourselves a *great* first day of school."

CHAPTER 4

I was *still* purring at the thought of how I would start my own battle academy.

How could I not have thought of this evil scheme sooner?

Rather than wasting my exile on this miserable barren rock of a planet, I could be training an elite fighting force! Then, when Flooffee-Fyr brought me home to Lyttyrboks, I would have my own loyal soldiers to do my merciless bidding—soldiers who would *never* betray me.

Naturally I would punish Flooffee-Fyr for his faithless stupidity. But I would save the worst of my rage for General Ffangg, who had been the *first* cat to overthrow me and exile me across the universe.

Flooffee was a mere annoyance—Ffangg was my true enemy.

His deceit was especially irritating, as I myself had raised him, turning him from a mewling orphaned kitten into the greatest general in all the one hundred billion galaxies.

While cats are not known for their loyalty, his betrayal, I felt, was too much.

I purred as I imagined the humiliating punishments he had surely been undergoing.

The shaving of his tail fur.

The clipping of his whiskers.

Baths.

I got up from the patch of sunlight and put my enormous brain toward the task at hand: recruitment.

Of course I would not bother myself with this planet's lower life-forms, such as Humans. The soldiers I sought were the cats of Earth.

CHAPTER 5

I got lost on the way to math and was so late that I had to sit in the back row, miles away from Cedar and so far from the board that I couldn't decide if I needed glasses or binoculars.

After going the wrong way twice, I made it to science, and after going the wrong way *three* times, I got to English. I was late, of course, so I didn't get to sit next to Steve. In fact, I had to stand. What kind of school didn't have enough *chairs*?

My stomach rumbled all the way through social studies, and I was totally dehydrated because none of the drinking fountains worked. By the time I got to gym, I was so light-headed from hunger and thirst that I almost passed out playing volleyball.

When the bell rang, I sprinted to lunch. This was

the one period I could **not** be late for. Nothing is worse than getting to a packed cafeteria and having no place to sit, no matter *what* day of school it is.

So it was a relief to get to the cafeteria and see that most of the tables were still empty. But then I saw . . . THE LINE.

It was at least seventy-five kids long, and I was the last one in it. I watched as kid after kid came out with a tray of food and promptly filled up another seat in the cafeteria. A seat that could have been mine.

By the time I got into the room with the hot plates, I was too nervous to be hungry. Maybe that was a good thing, since the only vegetarian option was a pile of floppy carrot sticks.

When I made it back to the lunchroom, the only table left with any space was the worst one of all.

The cool kids' table.

Gulp.

CHAPTER 6

Though I previously held the cats of Earth in low regard, I had come to realize that they were not simply the idiotic, language-less fools they appeared to be.

Somewhere in the haze of their Earth-cat brains lurked a stunted but functional feline intelligence. The evidence for this lay in how they had tricked their ogres into serving them. Their ploys ranged from staging hunger strikes to gain the most delicious food to meowing relentlessly until Humans used their club-like opposable thumbs to open a closed door.

Most remarkably, they had gotten Humans to scratch, pet, and massage them, all for the reward of a purr—a sound that every feline knows conveys triumph and gloating. They mocked their ogres even while being served by them!

Purr!

Using these Earth-cat techniques, I had trained my own Humans. These days I only occasionally scratched them, as acts of random violence kept them on their toes.

(But never the mother-Human. One must beware around mother-Humans.)

As for which Earth cat would have the luck of being my first recruit, I needed to look no farther than out the front window of my fortress.

The Flabby Tabby.

I strolled across the street to greet him, slipping in through a narrow opening underneath the garage door. The obese one was perched upon his windowsill, snoozing. He sensed my presence—at least he was alert—and his eyes went round. He fled.

Resistance, my fleshy friend, is futile.

I caught Flabby easily. Using the trap-and-lead device the ogres call a "leash," I dragged him across the street and into my underground bunker. He immediately took shelter under a couch and refused to come out.

My next (and more promising) prospect was the orange she-cat who lived to the rear of my fortress. Orange females are rare on Lyttyrboks—and, one must assume, on this wretched planet as well—but they are known to be admirably vicious.

This one followed me willingly back to the bunker. In fact, she appeared ready to do whatever I commanded.

I was already halfway to victory!

Their soft minds would easily absorb my training techniques, and the reeducation process would go forth with ease. By week's end, I would have the beginnings of a feline fighting force such as this sorry world had never *seen*.

CHAPTER 7

I took a deep breath and sat down in the last remaining place at the table. But I only put *one* butt cheek on the bench so I didn't crowd the kid next to me. Maybe, just maybe, he wouldn't even notice I was there.

He didn't say anything, but he did shoot me a disgusted look. Then he took an enormous bite of his hamburger.

The kid across the table from me, though, leaned in and looked at my tray. He had blond hair, pink cheeks, and big hipster glasses.

"Where's your lunch?" he said.

I held up a carrot stick.

"Are you a rabbit?" he said.

Like I'd never heard *that* one before. "I'm a vegetarian," I said.

"I'm a Max," he said, eyeing me a little suspiciously. "I've never seen you before. Did you go to *Upper* Elba Elementary?"

"No, I just moved here over the summer," I said. Then I added, "From Brooklyn."

"Really? The Big Apple?" he asked. "The City That Never Sleeps?"

I nodded. "Yeah. No one really calls it those things, though."

"That is so cool!" he said.

And immediately, everyone at the table looked friendlier—even the hamburger kid. They all started talking at once.

"Brooklyn! Is that where the Brooklyn Bridge is?" "And Coney Island?" "I've *always* wanted to go to New

York City." "I heard there's more rats than people." "Do you have grass there?" "What's Times Square like?" "Have you ever been mugged?" "Is it dangerous?" "Are there famous people everywhere?" "Do you know any famous people?"

No one had ever been this interested in me before— let alone six people at once.

Max repeated the last question. "Yeah, do you know any famous people?"

I thought for a minute. "I know a famous writer," I said.

The burger kid—whose real name was Brody— laughed. "There's no such thing."

"Zoe Addams," I said, shrugging.

Everyone stopped eating and stared at me.

"She's, uh, the lady who wrote Americaman," I said.

"We *know* who Zoe Addams is," Max said, and even Brody was nodding excitedly.

Everyone at the table opened their backpack and took out an Americaman book. Together they had the whole ten-book series, two times over.

"How do *you* know her?" Brody asked skeptically.

I had to think about how to answer for a second. "Um, her son, Cameron—he's my best friend," I said. "I practically used to live at their house in Brooklyn."

Okay, this was not totally true—Cam *wasn't* my best friend, at least not anymore. But it was too complicated to explain right now, and it wasn't like I'd ever get called on it. Cam lived three thousand miles away.

"In the back of *Americaman* #7 there's an interview with Zoe Addams that says she uses people she knows as characters in her books," Max said. "Are *you* in any of her books?"

"Yeah," Brody said, a little threateningly. "*Are* you?"

As a matter of fact, I was. And *that* was 100 percent true.

"You know the one where Americaman's sidekick, Starsey Stripes, saves a kid from being crushed by the evil self-driving Overlift car? That kid," I said with a shrug, "is me."

Brody scowled. "That was in #6," he said, reaching across the table to grab it from Max. He flipped to the right page and pointed to the panel where the kid thanks Starsey Stripes for saving his life. "You mean to tell me that this is you?"

I nodded.

"It *does* look like him," one of the girls at the table said.

"Whoa!" Max said, clapping his hands. "Brooklyn is the COOLEST!"

And all at once, the table exploded. *Everyone* wanted to talk to me. One kid even wanted me to sign his comic!

Maybe middle school wasn't going to be so bad after all.

CHAPTER 8

"Good morning, Earth cats," I said in my most majestic voice. "Welcome to Wyss-Kuzz's Warrior Academy! Here you will learn the ancient philosophies of battle, the science of weapons engineering, the art of deceit, and—best of all—the greatest system of martial arts in the known universe: **Mew-Jytzu.**"

My students blinked at me, their faces as blank as blackest space.

I approached the ginger she-cat. "I will begin with you," I said, and unsheathed my claws.

A mind-meld would allow me to quickly understand her thoughts.

"Consider this an aptitude test."

But I had barely touched my claws to her forehead before I was bombarded with images of food cans, feathery toys, and pillowy cat beds. I pulled back instantly. Her mind was a garbage dump of inanity!

I glanced over at the Flabby Tabby, who was licking his own—"STOP THAT, you vile Earth cat!"

I would not be peering into the dark recesses of *his* brain.

It appeared that I would have to take things more slowly than anticipated. To this end, I decided to begin with lessons that any feline should grasp by the time they grow their second whiskers—general relativity, electromagnetism, and biochemistry. I expected no comprehension problems here.

I sketched out some of the most basic equations in the universe, but when I turned back to my pupils, I saw that Flabby Tabby was asleep, and Ginger was staring at me, her head cocked to the side. It appeared to me that she had never even *seen* elementary calculus before. What had her mother taught her when she was nursing?

"Mrow?"

"No talking!" I said. "Pay attention."

I brought out a large piece of cardboard. The humans utilized this material to make boxes—one of their more advanced products—but I now used it to scratch out the glorious alphabet of Lyttyrboks. Or, at least, the principal 1,392 characters that all kittens must master while still in the litter.

When I had finished, I let Ginger try her paw at writing an essay. She scratched and kneaded at the cardboard expertly. She was a genius! I had *never* seen a cat compose with such speed. Brown shreds went flying up into the air.

We would now be able to communicate. As my new second-in-command, she would help me recruit *other* Earth cats!

When she was finished, I inspected what she had scratched out.

It was utter gibberish!

"*Mrow*?" Ginger said.

Flabby Tabby opened one eye. "Mrow?" he echoed.

I paced the room, swishing my tail. These cats were
imbeciles!

It was time for a *new* evil plan.

Luckily, I had an inkling of what that would be.

CHAPTER 9

Even though I was still really hungry, I left the cafeteria happy. There was only one last class to get through.

I found my way to the mysterious Lab RBX, where Cedar and Steve had saved me a seat. I was just about to sit down at the worktable when I felt a slap on my back.

"Hey, losers!"

It was Scorpion, the mean kid from Camp Eclipse. He looked like he was going to slap me again—maybe this time on my head—but then our teacher walked in.

Was that our teacher? She had tattoos up and down both arms, a bunch of hoops in her ears, and long black hair dyed red at the ends.

"Everybody take a seat," she said, looking directly at Scorpion and Newt, who stuck her tongue out at me.

Then something crazy happened. There was an

extra chair at our table, and all of a sudden there were two kids trying to sit in it.

So they could be next to *me*.

"Hey, can *I* have this chair?" Max asked.

"Outta the way, dude," Brody said. "I sit next to Brooklyn."

I didn't know what to say! But the teacher did.

"This is not a social event, Bookworms," she said firmly. "You two go sit at that empty table. Now that we're all settled, my name is Miss Natasha, and this is Robotics 101."

Robotics? I *loved* robotics! This was the best day of school ever!

Miss Natasha crossed her arms and gazed at us all. "What do alfalfa farming, dentistry, and online shopping orders have in common?" she asked.

Cedar raised her hand. "Um, robots?"

"Exactly!" Miss Natasha said. "A farmer can use a robot to harvest crops. A robot recently gave a patient two new teeth. And a robot fetches online orders from warehouse shelves." She raised an eyebrow at us. "Pretty cool, huh?"

It wasn't just cool. Robotics was the coolest thing ever! Miss Natasha didn't need to sell *me* on it. I'd been doing robotics after school since I was eight. In fact, it's where I met Cameron. We were robot buddies.

Back before we were enemies, that is.

Max raised his hand. "Are robots going to do everything that we used to do?"

"Some people are worried that robots will take over the world," she said.

"That'd be so cool!" Scorpion said.

"What's *true* is that robots—be they vacuum cleaners or spaceships—are only a tool," Miss Natasha said. "They are as good or bad as the humans who make them." She smiled. "Needless to say, we will spend our time making *good* robots. In fact, that's our project for this section—to make robots that will help our school. The team that makes the bot that best fits our goals will have the opportunity to demonstrate it to the community at the Wormy Apple Harvest Festival next month."

"The what?" I whispered to Cedar, who was nearly bouncing up and down with excitement.

"The Harvest Festival! It's like this awesome county fair, but at our school," Cedar said.

Steve didn't look so excited. He looked actually worried. "Could robots *really* take over the world?" he asked.

Cedar patted his huge shoulder. "If they do, it'll be long after we're dead," she told him.

Oddly, that seemed to make Steve feel better.

"Each worktable will be a team, and each team will build their creations from components they can find back *here*," Miss Natasha said. She slid open a folding divider in the back of the lab to reveal a storeroom of robot parts.

"Ooooh!" the class all went.

"As a team, you must decide on a basic robot body—stationary, rolling, or hover drone. From there, you may add on any number of attachment parts—arms with pincers, lights, sound players, and so forth. But it's up to you what good deed your robot will do. Will it sharpen pencils? Will it clean blackboards? Will it be a companion for a shy child? Points will be awarded for ideas and execution. Use of recycled parts found *outside* of the lab are worth extra credit. So, start brainstorming. Dream big, Bookworms!"

Cedar grinned at me. "This is going to be *awesome*."

For once, I agreed.

CHAPTER 10

It was late in the Earth day—long after I had sent Flabby Tabby and Ginger back to their own fortresses—when the boy-Human returned and found me in the belowground bunker.

"Did you learn how to eat today?" I asked.

He failed to grasp my biting wit. All he wanted to talk about was how he had made *friends*.

Friends? What did that word even *mean*?

But he did bring news of some interest to me. He was taking a class in robotics. No doubt whatever machine he built would be extremely primitive, but it did mean that his school might not be a *complete* waste of time.

Not that what the boy-Human studied mattered to me. I did not need his skills. I needed something else entirely.

Kittens.

The Human continued his blathering, but I could no longer even pretend to listen.

"Where might one acquire a kitten?" I interrupted. "Perhaps even an entire litter of them?"

"Kittens? Oh, that's easy," the boy-Human said. "There are kittens up for adoption all the time!"

"Ah, yes, *adoption*!" I said. "How does one do this 'adoption'?"

"I'll show you." The Human opened his "laptop," the flat box he used to access cyberspace via a cumbersome system of finger-pecking. As if it couldn't be done more simply using brain waves!

After an interminable number of seconds, he found something called PetSeeker. On the screen I saw pictures of *hundreds* of kittens.

What sort of a world was this? Were all of these kittens ripped from their mothers and littermates and destined to live with these awful Humans?

On the other paw, this was a prospective *legion* of suckling soldiers at my clawtips!

"It must be extremely expensive to 'adopt' one of these kittens," I said.

"Not really," the boy-ogre said. "Most people give kittens away for free."

For free? This was appalling! Humans, I knew, were paid by the hour—and yet a cat's entire *lifetime of service* was deemed worthless?

"Aw, look at these three," the boy-Human said, pointing at the screen. "They live right down our street."

My whiskers twitched in excitement as we watched a video of two playful gray boy-cats. Then—out of nowhere—a ferocious she-calico leaped into the screen and began positively pummeling them.

"Why are you asking, Klawde?" the boy-Human said. "Are you lonely?"

I considered scratching him for such an absurd suggestion. "What you call 'loneliness' the cats of Lyttyrboks call the highest, purest state of being," I said.

I pushed the ogre aside and peered more closely at the screen. This was it: the true beginning of my elite fighting force.

Purrrrrrrrr.

CHAPTER 11

My mom, wearing her lab coat as an apron, was sautéing onions when I came bursting in the kitchen door.

"You'll never believe it," I told her. "School wasn't terrible at *all*!"

"That's wonderful, dear," she said, stirring the pot. "I hope your teachers gave you lots of homework."

I assured her that they had, and then I told her all about robotics class and the kids I'd met, and when I had run out of things to say, she told me that she had some news, too.

"We got the grant I applied for, which funds an additional position at the lab," she said. "The new person starts in two weeks!"

Now why would I care about *that*?

"By the way, Raj," she said, "have you heard from your old friend Cameron yet?"

Cameron! Why did he keep coming up? And what did she mean by *yet*?

I told Mom I had definitely *not* heard from Cam and went upstairs to my room, where Klawde was napping on my beanbag. I sat down next to him and sighed.

"Please, do not tell me what is bothering you," he said.

"It's just that it's *weird*," I said. "Getting away from Cameron was the one good thing about leaving

Brooklyn, but it's like there's no way to escape him."

"Fascinating," Klawde said, closing his eyes.

I told him about how Cam and I had been best friends from the moment we met in the Bots-4-Tots program at Brooklyn Robot Factory. We loved all the same things: everything bagels, basketball, board games, and superhero comics. *Especially* superhero comics. Stuff like Batman, X-Men, and Americaman, which back then was a web comic nobody had even heard about. But we didn't care—Cam's *mom* drew it! Every year, we'd dress up like Americaman and Starsey Stripes and go to Comic-Con with Mrs. Addams.

"Klawde, are you still alive?" I said, poking him.

"Unfortunately," he mumbled.

Things changed when the first Americaman book got published, and the comic suddenly got huge. It was awesome!

The only downside was that Cameron's head started

getting kind of huge, too. Since Americaman's sidekick, Starsey Stripes, was based on him, Cameron would get interviewed alongside his mom for podcasts and articles, and he was all over YouTube. Nobody thought he was dorky anymore (even though he still wore a cape to recess sometimes) and everyone wanted to be his friend. And pretty soon he was acting like he was too good for everybody at school.

Including me.

I tried to ignore it. Comic-Con was coming up again, and I couldn't wait to go with my best friend and his megastar mom. I'd been working on my costume for weeks. But when I brought it to school to show Cam, he looked at me like I was crazy.

"I'm not taking *you*, Raj," he'd said. "I'm taking Bronco Jones."

It was the worst news I'd ever heard. Bronco Jones thought he was the coolest kid in Brooklyn—which he kind of was—but he hadn't even known Cam *existed* six months earlier.

"I mean, sorry or whatever," Cam had said. "But the Bronc is my best friend."

Since *when*?

And to make things even worse, Cam told everyone that I'd cried when he said I couldn't go.

I didn't tell him that I knew he'd talked behind my back. What was the point? He was a jerk, and I didn't want to be friends with a jerk. It didn't matter how famous his mom was.

So it was pretty ironic that I was popular at my new school because of Cam.

Actually, it didn't feel ironic—it just felt wrong.

"Try accidentally blowing up a planet or two before telling me what 'feels wrong,'" Klawde said.

I stared at him. He *had* to be making some of this stuff up, right?

"Anyway," he said, "the Humans at your pitiful school like you. Isn't that what you wished for?" He flexed a claw. "If only you could understand that fear is superior to affection."

I realized that Klawde had a good point. I shouldn't let Cam ruin how great my first day of school was. I could hardly wait for tomorrow!

CHAPTER 12

The boy-Human practically skipped out of bed in the morning. (This was unusual. He normally seemed incapable of facing the universe.) He ate his breakfast quickly—feeding me half his fried egg and a pat of butter, as I had trained him—and hurried out the door to his school.

The mature ogres also left for their daytime activities, though with somewhat less enthusiasm. As soon as they were gone, I slipped out the front door and made haste to the address listed on PetSeeker.

I found the kittens in a small outbuilding behind the main fortress, napping beneath a collection of instruments which, I assumed, were designed for various acts of violence.

The mother cat slunk out of the shadows and hissed at me.

"Hello, madam," I said. "My name is Wyss-Kuzz, and I come to you this morning as a recruiter for intergalactic warriors."

She tilted her head to one side and blinked.

"May I meet your children?"

She yawned, lay down, and closed her eyes.

I took that as a yes.

"Wake, young ones!" I said, walking over to their napping place. "It is time to meet your destiny!"

The two gray boys looked at me sleepily. The calico girl, however, launched herself at my face! Only my lightning-quick reflexes allowed me to dodge her attack.

I liked her already.

I turned to their mother. "Your children show great potential. May I take them under my claw? I would like them to be the first class in my new training academy."

She didn't bother looking up. One of the boys went to nurse and she swatted him away. Clearly she was ready to wean them.

I reached out a paw and touched the calico she-kitten's head. This rudimentary mind-meld told me all I needed to know: The minds of these kittens were still free of Human corruption.

These little creatures could be *taught*.

The two boys now went to play with their sister, who swatted them both with one blow. Soon all three were viciously tackling each other. They possessed more fighting spirit than I had seen in any other creature on this planet.

"Young cadets!" I cried. "Follow me!"

They seemed to understand my language—another

first—and were most pleased to do as I asked.

Well, they *started* doing as I asked. But after following me into the yard, one of the boys ran off after a butterfly and the other scampered halfway up a tree and then hung there, mewing pitifully. The calico, on the other paw, began stalking a squirrel.

I snatched her by the scruff of her neck and held her in my jaws in Vanquished Prey position.

As all kittens do, she immediately surrendered into serene calmness. I began walking to the fortress again, and her brothers followed obediently behind me.

As I held her neck between my teeth, I remembered the last time I held a young kit in my maw, oh so many years ago. **Ffangg**.

I would *not* repeat the mistakes I had made with him. I would create soldiers that would never—*could* never—turn against me.

CHAPTER 13

So far the second day of school was going even better than the first.

After taking attendance, Miss Emmy Jo spent the rest of homeroom showing us pictures of her miniature horse. "Isn't Gummy Bear just the cutest little muffin top y'all have ever seen?"

He kind of was.

At lunch, the cool kids *invited* me to their table. One of them even got up to give me his seat. It was like I had entered some kind of alternate dimension.

They kept asking about living in New York, and I started to exaggerate some. It was hard not to with an audience like this—they kept begging for more! So I told them about the time our house got broken into. (It was actually just our downstairs neighbor's dog walker coming into our apartment by mistake.) And I told them about sitting next to the mayor on the F train. (Okay, it was probably just a guy who looked like him. But he really, *really* looked like him!)

Even what should have been the worst moment of the day turned out well. In the hallway, I bumped into an eighth-grade girl by mistake. Hard. She was a foot taller than me and about ten times as cool, and I'd just made her spill her bottle of water all down her dress.

"Are you the new kid?" she asked.

I nodded in fear. "Sorry?"

"Is it true you were in *Americaman: Killer Kar 4 Hire*?"

"Uh, yeah?" I said.

Then she smiled. At me! "Cool. See you around."

I walked into robotics with the biggest grin in the world.

"I hope you all have arrived brimming with good

ideas," Miss Natasha said. "Discuss them with your team and then begin selecting components in the back of the lab. After that, we'll reconvene to discuss what you've come up with."

Newt and Scorpion immediately dove into the pile of parts. Newt was fast, and she grabbed a brand-new drone and held it over her head triumphantly.

Steve's face fell. "*I* wanted that drone," he said.

"We're supposed to figure out what we're going to do first," Cedar reminded him.

As we talked, Scorpion snatched the controls away from Newt and piloted the drone straight into a wall.

"So what can we do that's going to help the school?" Cedar asked.

Steve scrunched up his face like he was thinking really hard. It looked painful.

"How about a robot that builds chairs?" I suggested. I was only half kidding. (Standing through English was seriously tiring.) But then I had a *great* idea.

"I know!" I said. "Since none of the water fountains in this school ever work, how about we make a robot that gives out water?"

Cedar and Steve looked at me like I was stupid. After I quickly sketched out my concept, though, Cedar nodded and said, "I like it."

"But will it try to take over the world?" Steve asked. "Like that self-driving car in Americaman?"

"*No,*" Cedar and I both said.

When Miss Natasha asked everyone to talk about their robots, I got up and explained our plan. Our robot would roam the halls of school, dispensing water through a faucet appendage. "It will eliminate waste from plastic bottles," I said, "and promote good hydration."

"Very good, Raj! Excellent idea," Miss Natasha said. Then she turned to Scorpion. "What about your team?"

Scorpion grinned. "You know how Principal Brownepoint hates it when kids wear their pants too low? Well, our drone's going to go around and help kids pull their pants up. It's called the Butt-bot."

The entire class started laughing. Except Miss Natasha.

"I'm going to suggest you rethink your goal *and* your robot's name," she said. "Because if a drone reached for my waistband, I'd slap it right out of the sky."

CHAPTER 14

The second day of Wyss-Kuzz's Warrior Academy went markedly better with the new recruits.

After my initial experience teaching Earth cats, I decided to dispense with the sciences and high-level mathematics altogether. The kittens had already missed too much of the basics to catch up. Besides, they were going to be warriors, not philosophers. The only geometry they needed to learn was the trajectory of a pounce!

After allowing them some open battle time, I assembled my recruits for an inspiring speech. I quoted liberally from *Battle Is the Most Magnificent Competition in Which a Cat Can Indulge*, the ancient text I had memorized when I was six weeks old.

"Cadets!" I cried. "Since the dawn of time, when primitive cats first marked trees with their claws and filled the night with their yowls, we have understood

a very basic truth: Each cat is his own master. But!"

I cleared my throat, and the kittens blinked. "*Some* cats

are more masterful than others."

The boys seemed to struggle to comprehend;

the calico, on the other paw, nodded in agreement. I

continued my inspiring lecture until the sun was high

in the sky, and ended with the immortal words of the

original warmonger, Myttynz the Mrowdyr: *There is*

no nobler pastime than vanquishing your enemies.

The kittens lapped it up! Then we did battle ball drills.

For snack time, I presented the kittens with the

insipid brown pellets the Humans insisted on leaving

out for me. They devoured them all.

After a brisk focus nap, I demonstrated the nine

fundamental poses of Mew-Jytzu and concluded the

day with a sparring session. The gray twins fought each

other to a tie. Their form was quite sloppy.

"No, no! You must strike with your claws *extended*!" I hissed.

The calico needed no such pointers. She dispatched each of her brothers so quickly that, for the final match, I paired both boys against her. The fight was even, until one of the grays caught the calico with a strike to the head that sent her sliding across the floor. She crouched in a corner, meowing pitifully. Had she been injured? Had I overestimated her fighting skills?

The boys went to check on the state of their sister. Once they were near, the girl sprang forward with a leap so lightning-fast, they had no time to react. She landed on their backs, slashing and biting and yowling with glee.

By Lyttyrboks's eighty-seven moons, this calico was a fierce warrior! So fierce, in fact, that she reminded me of the greatest warrior I had ever encountered.

Myself.

CHAPTER 15

At breakfast, Klawde came up for his egg and butter and immediately disappeared again. It had been like this for a week or two. He'd been acting stranger than ever, and sometimes I heard crazy sounds coming from downstairs. Crazier than usual, I mean.

I wondered if he was feeling okay. There was certainly a lot of poop in the litter box these days—what happened to him using the toilet?

I would talk to him this afternoon, even if that meant not staying so late after school working on the robot in the RBX Lab. Steve had been begging me and Cedar for a break anyway.

In homeroom, Miss Emmy Jo showed us videos from her most recent miniature horse show.

"And *this* is me leading Gummy Bear over a

jumping course! Can you BELIEVE how high that little corn dog can jump?"

In truth, it wasn't very high at all. What was more impressive was Miss Emmy Jo trotting alongside of him in her glittering denim jumpsuit. How could she *run* with all those sequins on?

The rest of the day was just me making it through my classes until I got to robotics. I'd never looked forward to a class so much before.

The parts Miss Natasha had were amazing—way better than what we'd had at Brooklyn Robot Factory. And everything was totally plug-and-play, like Legos almost.

We'd chosen a rolling chassis for our robot's main body. Cedar had the genius idea of sticking recycled, sterilized water bottles to the outside shell so kids could pull them off and re-use them.

We'd gotten a recorder so our robot could have a

voice. And then there were the sounds the buttons made.

This was Steve's contribution. We rigged up the carbon dioxide canister from his parents' old Fizz-Master so kids could have sparkling water. They could choose *how* sparkling by pressing buttons for how much gas to add. They were marked:

REGULAR

FIZZY

SUPER-FIZZY

MEGA-**FIZZY**

But they could've been labeled *no fart, farty, super-farty,* and *mega-farty* because that was the sound they made with each release of gas. Steve laughed every time he pressed one.

Every time.

The last thing we needed to work out were the spigots, which were old water pistols connected to hoses. This was *my* idea.

The Aqua-Bot looked **SO COOL!**

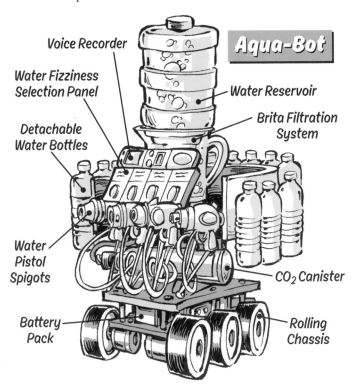

Voice Recorder

Water Fizziness
Selection Panel

Detachable
Water Bottles

Water
Pistol
Spigots

Battery
Pack

Aqua-Bot

Water Reservoir

Brita Filtration
System

CO₂ Canister

Rolling
Chassis

Scorpion and Newt's drone, on the other hand,
looked like a pile of debris. It had one robot arm and a
scary-looking pincer thing that was supposed to open and
close but was permanently stuck halfway in between.

"Hey, Brooklyn," Scorpion called to me.

I was amazed he was calling me by my cool new nickname, *and* in a tone like he didn't want to kill me.

"Could you . . . *uh* . . . well . . ." Scorpion hemmed and hawed.

"He wants you to help us with this pincer thingie," Newt said.

It took me only about ten seconds to find the problem, and another five minutes to fix it. Now the robot's pincer opened and shut with a *clack*.

"Wow," Newt said. "Maybe you're not a loser after all."

"Yeah," Scorpion added. "Maybe not."

"Were they actually nice to you?" Cedar asked when I got back to our table.

"Robots have taken them over," Steve said. "It's the only explanation."

CHAPTER 16

Today was a most important day. The first thirteen sunrises of Wyss-Kuzz's Warrior Academy for Kitten Commandos had gone supremely well. The boys had completed the basics of Mew-Jytzu and were ready to graduate to Star Paw level. The calico, however, had already qualified for advanced Nova Paw certification.

This amazed me. Not even Ffangg had reached Nova Paw so quickly.

For the ceremony, we had an audience, as Ginger and Flabby Tabby had both been frequenting the bunker lately: Ginger because she liked to spar, and Flabby because he had nothing better to do.

After the ritualistic rubbing of cheeks and slash of the claw, I spoke a few words about the bright future all three kittens had as the nucleus of my elite force.

And then it was time to eat. For myself only, however. The kittens had to wait until the Humans slept, and even then were allowed only the brown pellets for sustenance. A soldier must get used to spartan rations.

Upstairs, I performed the usual charade of begging for food. I did my best impression of an annoying Earth cat, mewling and howling until they served me.

"Stop it, Klawde!" the mother-Human said, putting down a bowl for me. "My eardrums are going to start bleeding!"

Ah, if only!

The food was *indeed* delicious this night, a warm liquid combination of milk, butter, and something pink.

"You like that tomato bisque, do you, boy?" the father-Human said. "And with all the kibble you've been eating, too! You better watch the midnight binge-eating—you don't want to get tubby!"

"Look who's talking," the mother-Human said.

The father-Human patted his belly as if he were proud of it, and that was when I heard it: the high-pitched mewing! The sound was not coming from down in the bunker—it was *much closer*.

The young warriors were coming up the stairs!

"Do I hear . . . ?" the boy-Human began to say.

"It's nothing!" I said. I was so quick to cut him off, however, that I forgot to pretend that I couldn't speak their imbecilic tongue.

The room fell silent.

Raj and I looked at each other. The boy-Human's face filled with fear.

"Did Klawde just . . . ," the father-ogre said. *"Talk?"*

"Don't be ridiculous," the mother-ogre said. "His brain functions at only a slightly higher level than that gargantuan fern you brought home."

"But I could swear he said . . ." The bald ogre thought for a second, his puny brain trying to process what he'd just heard. Finally he gave up.

"Mrow?" I said.

"See?" the mother-Human said. "Houseplant. With vocal cords."

My disguise safe, I raced to the bunker steps. The kittens were almost at the top, sniffing their way toward the food! The calico, of course, was leading the way.

I quickly snatched her up in Vanquished Prey position and whisked her down to the bunker. Thankfully, the simple-minded boys followed. Once I spit her into the cardboard box where they slept, I tossed the boys in, too.

"A soldier must have patience!" I scolded them. "You must be able to control such base desires as hunger!"

The calico bit me.

She was a true fighter.

Then:

"Klawde?"

It was the boy-Human's voice. He was coming down the stairs!

"Is there another cat down here?" the boy-ogre said. "I heard *normal* meowing."

"NO! Absolutely not!" I said. "I am only practicing the . . . the . . . the barbaric language of Earth cats."

The gullible ogre might have believed me. Might have, that is, had the calico not come bounding out of her sleep-box and attacked the laces of the boy-Human's foot coverings.

"*What . . . ,*" he said, "is **this**?"

At that, the two boys leaped out.

The jig was up!

What would happen now? Knowing this boy-ogre's do-good instincts—his absurd "morals"—he would insist on returning them.

What could I do? He was now holding all *three* of them in that ogreish death grip of his. I was terrified of what he would do to my precious recruits.

"I don't care about anything else in this world, Klawde," he said, his eyes wide and full of wonder. "But we **must** keep these kittens!"

Purrrrr.

CHAPTER 17

Just when I thought life couldn't get any better:
kittens!

Three of them!

I could not believe how cute they were. All weekend
long, I played with them down in the basement.

"Stop with your accursed affection!" Klawde said.
"You are going to turn them into soft Earth cats with all
this 'petting'!"

The two gray ones, maybe. But the calico—she was
like some sort of demon. I was a little afraid of her. My
shins and arms already looked like scratching posts.

I still didn't quite understand how Klawde had
managed to adopt them. And why did he want three
kittens anyway?

"Er, um, well . . . ," he said. "It is because of that

lonely thing you were talking about. Yes! I am *lonely*."

I was pretty sure Klawde was lying.

But I didn't care, because—again—**KITTENS**!·

Plus, I hadn't been exactly 100 percent truthful myself lately.

Kids at school kept wanting to know more about my Americaman connection, and I sort of started exaggerating that, too. Like how I used to watch Mrs. Addams draw stuff—which was true—and how I would suggest plots to her—also true—and how she would take my suggestions—*not* true. She always said she was going to use my ideas, but she never did.

I also kind of implied that Cam and I texted every day, and that I might be featured in the next Americaman book.

It wasn't like I meant to lie. It just sort of happened.

Like I sort of happened not to mention the kittens to my parents.

But knowing I wasn't being totally honest with everyone made me feel guilty. And like somehow I was going to get caught.

So on Monday, when Brody said there was a new kid at school from New York City, I felt a stab of panic.

"Hey, Raj, maybe you'll know him!" Max said.

And then I realized how ridiculous it was to worry. I laughed. "There are, like, nine million people in New York. There's no way I'm going to know him!"

I was just sitting down at my worktable next to Cedar and Steve when Miss Natasha began class with an announcement.

"Class," she said, "I would like to introduce you to our new student."

When I turned around, I just about fell off my chair.

Because I *did* know him.

And he was the **last** kid on Earth I wanted to see.

CHAPTER 18

Disaster had been narrowly averted with the boy-ogre. Thank the eighty-seven moons he was terrified of the mother-Human and willing to cooperate in my deception. Perhaps there was hope for him yet.

Still, I awoke with disquiet. My whiskers trembled, and I sensed a disturbance in the space-time continuum. I had first felt it yesterday, but it was much stronger now.

I tried to ignore it as I took the boys into the yard to begin acquainting them with intermediate Mew-Jytzu. When they napped in the grass, I taught the calico more advanced moves. I was in the middle of demonstrating the Flying Razor Slash on Flabby Tabby—he was useful as a tackling dummy—when my whiskers began to positively quiver.

Something was wrong.

Then I heard a loud buzzing.

It was the intergalactic communicator!

I pounced on it and looked to see who was calling.

MISERABLE TWO-FACED LACKEY.

It was Flooffee-Fyr! Finally!

I answered the phone triumphantly. "So, at last you call, you pathetic excuse for a feline."

"Oh, *hey*, former Lord High Emperor," Flooffee said. "I'm, uh, really glad I got through to you. I'm sure you're really busy there, like, avoiding carnivorous ogres and all."

"Enough with the small talk!" I said. "I know why you have contacted me."

"You DO?" he said.

"Yes," I proclaimed. "You have finally come to terms with your own ineptitude and have decided that you need me—the greatest warlord in the known universe!— to come replace you as Supreme Leader."

"Uhhhh . . . actually, I'm pretty *good* as Supreme Leader," he said. "I mean, I could do without all the violent uprisings and stuff, and it *is* hard to—"

"SILENCE!" I cried. "If you didn't contact me to bring me home, then *why* are you bothering me, you ignorant imbecile?"

"Well, it's, um, about the Council of Elders. You know how they are." Flooffee shook his head. "And, well, they've exiled another cat to Earth."

"WHAT?" I said. "That's impossible! No one but I could ever be wicked enough to deserve the ultimate punishment!"

"Hey, I told them, 'Elders, this is a total do-wrong,' but the prisoner requested it." Flooffee shook his head again. "I told the cat, 'Earth is **really** not the place you want to go . . .'"

"The prisoner requested it? *What* prisoner? Spit it out, you dim-witted dolt!"

Meanwhile the calico was trying to get my attention, pointing behind me, but I swatted her away.

"Tell me now, witless one!" I demanded. "WHO IS IT?"

"It is I, old friend," came a voice from behind me.

I whirled around.

And it was the **last** cat I wanted to see on Earth!

CHAPTER 19

CAMERON ADDAMS! *NOOOOOOOOOO!*

CHAPTER 20

GENERAL FFANGG! *HISSSSSSSSSSSS!*

CHAPTER 21

Cameron Addams.

I couldn't believe it! Why in the world was he here? How had my former best friend wound up in Oregon, in the exact same small-town school as me?

This had to be the biggest coincidence *ever*—and the worst one, too.

"Cameron just moved here last week," Miss Natasha told the class, "and his favorite hobby is building robots!"

I felt sick to my stomach. Now all the kids would find out that I'd exaggerated about helping with Americaman! Cam would tell everyone that his mom had never taken my advice, and that we were no longer best friends, and nobody would think that I was cool anymore. Then Cam would tell lies about me behind my back, and that would be *it* for me at Elba Middle School.

"So let's show him what we've done so far, class." Miss Natasha gestured to our table. "How about you guys go first?"

As Cedar, Steve, and I followed the rolling Aqua-Bot to the front of the room, Cam nodded hello to me, just like he used to do when we saw each other every day. Like he wasn't even surprised.

"So, uh, the Aqua-Bot here is, uh . . ." I couldn't think straight, I was so freaked out. "Well, it's supposed to, like, um, if you're thirsty, *well*—"

"The Aqua-Bot is a state-of-the-art hydration delivery system," Cedar said, coming to my rescue. "It is powered by lithium ion batteries, a series of Arduino processors, and human goodwill!" She smiled brightly as she grabbed the controller from me and guided our robot to Steve.

"*Are you* . . . THIRSTY?" the Aqua-Bot said as it lurched forward, lights blinking. Steve pressed the FIZZY button, and the Aqua-Bot extended one of its squirt gun arms. A narrow trickle of water dribbled out, splashing into the recycled plastic water bottle Steve was holding beneath it.

Frustrated, Steve kept pressing the buttons—SUPER-FIZZY, MEGA-FIZZY—but it wouldn't make the fart sounds. The hose from the CO_2 canister was probably loose again.

Nevertheless, Miss Natasha nodded encouragingly. "It looks like you have some fine-tuning to do, but that's a *great* start. Good job, you guys." Then she turned to Scorpion. "How's *your* robot coming along?" she asked.

Newt and Scorpion unveiled a hideous tangle of plastic parts and said, "Meet the Ro-butt!"

Miss Natasha's ears went pink. "Didn't we discuss this already?" she asked.

"But this is totally *different*!" Scorpion insisted. "It's not a Butt-bot, it's the Ro-butt, and the Ro-butt's job is to help kids sit down on their butts! Check it out!"

With Scorpion at the controller, the drone lifted a few feet into the air. Its long pincer arm dragged along on the floor as it hummed forward. Then the arm struggled upward and pulled out a chair for Newt to sit in.

At least, that's what it looked like. But Newt had hooked the leg of the chair with her foot, and I could tell she was really the one pulling it out.

"See? It works!" Scorpion said.

Newt and Scorpion both smiled big, proud smiles.

Miss Natasha was *not* impressed.

"Cameron," she said, "this team needs your help desperately. Will you please join them?"

"Sure," Cam said, shrugging.

Miss Natasha told us to get to work, and then the thing I was dreading happened.

Cam walked right up to me.

"Raj," he said, standing with his hands on his hips. "I was *wondering* when I'd run into you."

CHAPTER 22

"I see your tail is mightily puffed," Ffangg said. "Are you not happy to see your old friend?"

I hissed and spat into the grass. "You are not my friend! You are a mongrel-eyed milk-licker."

His own tail twitched slyly. "Ah, Wyss-Kuzz, always so hasty with the insult. Have you still not learned that it is better to be quick with the claw than fast with the tongue?"

I growled at his insolence. I would show him a quick claw!

"So, uh, I guess I'll be hanging up now," came the sound of Flooffee-Fyr's voice from the communicator. "You two must have a lot of catching up to do . . ."

"Flooffee, you moron!" I said, grabbing the phone. "How could you have allowed this to happen! I will pluck all your whiskers out! I will use your tail to wipe my—"

"*KSH-KSH!* Oh, hey, *what* did you say? The static is really bad all of a sudden! *KSH-KSH!*" Flooffee waved his paw in front of the screen. "You're breaking up. *KSH-KSH!* It's those last hundred thousand light-years— *really* tough on the signal . . . *KSH-KSH!*"

I went to yell at him again, but he had hung up.

"Oh, poor Wyss-Kuzz," Ffangg said. "You should have known that you are not the *only* cat evil enough to merit the ultimate punishment."

My blood began to boil like the cauldrons in which I cooked my enemies. "Exile was *my* punishment!" I thundered. "Must you copy **everything** I do?"

Ffangg ignored my question, further infuriating me. "This planet is a miserable place indeed," he said as he took in the walled training ground. "I can see why our ancestors chose it. Is it true that the Humans force you to play with stuffed animals for their amusement and steal your excrement with a small shovel?"

"You must go back to Lyttyrboks immediately!"

"Sadly, I cannot," Ffangg said. "The wormhole, you see, was opened only long enough to deposit me here. So how about we allow bygones to be bygones?" He bared his teeth at me in a gesture of friendship.

It was *grotesque*.

"Let us return to the days before our troubles began. Let us join *together*." Ffangg came close to me and spoke in a low hiss. "For together we can rise up and conquer our oppressors. Together, our evil warmongering will be . . . *eternal and unstoppable*!"

A purr rose in my throat.

Ffangg had come crawling back to me—just like I always knew he would! At last he had realized that he was nothing without me. (He would have to be punished for his transgressions, of course, but I could address that matter later.)

"You have finally returned to your senses, Ffangg," I said. "What joy it shall be to overthrow that simpering simpleton Flooffee-Fyr."

Ffangg nodded. "He must be vanquished."

"His whiskers clipped!" I said.

"His tail shaved!" Ffangg cried.

"And his fur cast upon the wind!" we shouted together.

Just like *old* times.

We purred. We were in complete agreement.

CHAPTER 23

"Oh—oh, hey, Cam!" I stammered. "What—what are you doing in Oregon?"

"My dad got a job here," he said. "Didn't you know?"

It was *so* Cam to expect people to know every detail of his life.

"So you *do* know the new kid! I was right," Max said, coming up to us. "Who is he?"

"Yeah, who is he, Brooklyn?" Brody said.

"Brooklyn?" Cam repeated. "They call you *Brooklyn*?"

"Uh, he's . . . that friend of mine I was telling you about," I said to Max and Brody. The words were painful. "The one whose mom . . . writes Americaman."

"Whoa! *You're* the one?" Max said to Cam.

"Dude, that is so **cool**!" Brody said.

"STUDENTS!" Miss Natasha said. "What have I told you about this not being a social event?"

Thank goodness for Miss Natasha.

But even though everyone went back to their tables, I couldn't concentrate on the Aqua-Bot anymore. Cameron Addams was *in my classroom*. And already, I could tell he was ruining everything. I could hear Scorpion and Newt being *nice* to him, and Cam talking about what a big deal his mom was and dropping all kinds of Americaman references, and—worst of all—Brody saying, "Raj didn't even know Cameron was moving here. Some best friends *they* are."

I looked back and saw Max nodding.

I wanted to crawl under a table and die.

As soon as the bell rang, I slunk out of class, ran home, and sat in my room all afternoon reading comics.

Anything but Americaman.

When Mom came back after work, she called me into the kitchen and asked how my day was. I told her it was the craziest day ever.

"Why's that, dear?" Mom asked, with that smile she saved for questions she already knew the answer to. But she couldn't know this one!

I dropped the bomb. "**Cameron Addams** moved to Elba!" I said. "He's in my class! Can you *believe* it?"

My parents looked at each other, and then they started grinning.

"We knew!" she said. "We wanted it to be a surprise!"

"What? **Wait**—how did you *know*?"

"Because I hired his father to work in my lab!" Mom said proudly.

Have you ever had the thought that you could actually *feel* the spinning of the Earth?

I could barely get out the words.

"So it's *your* fault Cam is here?" I said.

"Fault? What do you mean, fault? You've been talking about how much you miss your old Brooklyn pals since we moved, and Cameron is your best friend."

Didn't she know *anything*?

As I went back to my room, I heard her say, "What's the matter with *him*?"

CHAPTER 24

The kittens quietly observed me and Ffangg until the calico grew bored of our conversation and slunk away as if to nap. Then she turned, rose up behind her brothers on her hind legs, and crashed their skulls together.

The gray boys whirled around and counterattacked, for once their fury matching that of their sadistic sister.

"Very impressive," Ffangg said. "I must commend you on training such excellent young warriors. Though I landed here but seven naptimes ago, it has provided me ample time to observe the pathetic state of catkind on this planet."

Flabby Tabby, who had been hiding underneath a bush, came out and laid on his back, exposing his fat belly to the sun.

"Appalling," Ffangg said. Then he turned to me and his eyes flashed with spite. "It will indeed be satisfying to lead you and your young soldiers in a coup against Flooffee-Fyr!"

"**WHAT?**" I howled.

"I said it will be—"

"I heard you, you traitorous fleabag!" I roared. "*You* will not lead *me* to anything! I am the Supreme Leader!"

Ffangg chuckled. "Oh, Wyss-Kuzz—still overestimating yourself," he said. "Your belly is nearly as round as the one who suns himself!"

"My belly is as taut and muscular as ever!" I raged. "And even if it *were* rounder, it would only be on account of the mother-ogre being such an excellent chef."

"Ha! Your teeth have grown yellow and your eyes are dull. You are no leader, Wyss-Kuzz." He gazed pointedly at my girth. "But you would make fine cannon fodder."

"You stringy son of a street cat!" I yelled. "You weak-brained claw-biter!"

I crouched in preparation for Ffangg to pounce, but the general merely lifted a paw and licked it.

"Dear old Wyss-Kuzz," he said. "How could you say such things about a cat you raised from a suckling kitten?" He turned to my cadets. "Did you know? Your 'master' also trained *me*. And soon you shall learn the same lesson I did: Wyss-Kuzz is not the most evil warlord in the universe. **I** am."

This was too much! I pounced, but the traitor performed the Mega-Triple Helix—a twisting backward leap—and landed deftly atop the fence.

"It has been lovely chatting with you all," Ffangg said. "But I must be going. Ta-ta!"

I jumped up to the fence—which, it must be said, was higher than it looked—but Ffangg was gone.

"Yes! Run away, you coward!" I cried, and turned back to the kitten commandos. "You see? This is how vermin slink away when faced with their superior!"

In their faces, however, I could see that the seeds of doubt had been sown.

CHAPTER 25

After dinner, I went to find Klawde. He was the only person—I mean, cat—er, *being* I could talk to. Not that he was so great with sympathy, but he *was* always talking about his enemies, so maybe the arrival of mine would interest him.

He was down in the basement, crouched in the middle of a disaster area. There was shredded cardboard everywhere—could that possibly have once been a box?—as well as the chewed-up stump of the fern my dad had just bought.

Klawde did not look happy. So that made two of us.

"You would not *believe* what happened in school today," I said, sinking down into Dad's La-Z-Boy.

Klawde didn't say anything. He just stayed in his crouch.

I told him about my former best friend moving to town and how it was going to wreck my life. Everyone in school already thought he was the coolest. And not only was I less cool, I'd lied about still being friends with Cam just so I could *seem* cool. Which made me the *un*coolest.

Klawde still didn't say anything.

"Earth to Klawde," I said. "Are you listening?"

"Earth!" Klawde spat. "Home of carnivorous ogres and now my own mortal enemy!"

"What do you mean?" I asked.

"The most traitorous cat in the known universe is here, on this vile planet of yours!"

My mouth fell open. "No way! There's another space kitty?"

Klawde growled. "He is not a *space kitty*. He is my former pupil and sworn enemy, a perfidious feline of arrogance, malevolence, and malice. And those are his good qualities."

I didn't know what at least two of those words meant. "But, Klawde, that's so weird. The same thing happened to me! Your former friend and enemy, *my* former friend and enemy—they both just landed in Elba!"

"I fail to see the connection," Klawde said.

"But don't you—"

"Silence!" Klawde said. "Enough of your tiresome drivel. I must speak to my troops." Then he sat up and looked around wildly. "Where *are* my troops?"

"Your troops?" I said. "You mean the kittens?"

But Klawde only hissed and ran out of the room.

CHAPTER 26

From the moment Ffangg left, I felt disquiet. He had turned tail and run, true, but not before exposing my kitten commandos to his lying propaganda. During the day's final battle exercises, I could swear that they were eyeing me suspiciously.

He must not be allowed to sweep my troops out from under me. Not again!

I ordered them to nap without rations and set myself to stew over the situation.

To assuage my fury, I shredded a large cardboard box and dismembered the jagged plant the father-Human had "decorated" the bunker with. Didn't the fool know plants belonged outdoors?

And then—to make matters worse—the boy-Human came down the stairs, whining over his petty problems.

He droned on about how some other child-Human from his home city had arrived here. The poor ignoramus really had no idea how tiny his planet was! It was inevitable that these ogres would cross paths.

Then he had the audacity to link his situation to mine. It was absurd. Did *he* have an army at stake?

And that was when I noticed—the kittens! They were gone! Maybe Ffangg's words *had* infected them.

Hissss!

I raced into the combat room and scanned the piles of laundry. At first I didn't see them, but I could hear a small, hushed voice—the voice of the calico.

When our eyes met, she went silent.

A look of guilt fell over the faces of the gray boys. The face of the she-cat, on the other paw, betrayed nothing but cunning. She was planning something. Something evil.

I felt that mixture of pride and murderous rage that only a parent can feel.

CHAPTER 27

"Good morning, y'all! A little birdie told me that there's a new student at Elba Middle School," said Miss Emmy Jo in homeroom. "And I hear he's a bit of a celebrity."

"Americaman!" came a high-pitched voice. Then a little boy appeared onscreen, wearing a Starsey Stripes costume that was two sizes too small. *"Americaman!"*

"Isn't that just the most precious thing y'all have ever seen?" Miss Emmy Jo said. "Willy Lee wore that for Halloween last year, and he's barely taken it off since!"

The other kids laughed, but not me.

All I could think about was running into our new "celebrity."

I didn't see Cam that morning, but I felt like he was everywhere. All anyone was talking about was "the Americaman kid."

And then I got to the cafeteria.

The spot where I usually sat—the one next to Brody—was occupied. By Cameron. He was telling a story, and everyone was laughing. Then some kid in a Starsey Stripes T-shirt came over and took a selfie with his arm around Cam.

I got a pair of celery sticks with brown spots on them and sat on the floor with the other kids who couldn't find a table, which was uncomfortably close to where the cool kids sat.

Where *I* used to sit.

I could hear Cam talking about how when Americaman was just a web comic, he had told his mom that *he* should be Americaman's sidekick, and that was why she created Starsey Stripes.

"And I also gave her the idea for Americaman's Fist of Freedom."

Americaman's greatest weapon, the Fist of

Freedom? That was *not* Cameron's idea—and I knew it, because I'd been there when his mom thought of it. I wanted to stand up and shout *LIES*! But I didn't want to draw attention to myself.

I was relieved when the bell finally rang and I could get out of there. But Max spotted me as I was leaving.

"Oh, hey, Raj," he said. "I didn't even realize you were here."

Yeah, no kidding, I thought.

CHAPTER 28

" . . . and so the fearsome and ferocious Father of the Feline Gods, KroMus, ate all of his offspring, so that none would betray him. *The end.*"

Every naptime, I settled the kittens to sleep in the bunker with tales of Lyttyrboks lore. As with all young kits, they preferred stories filled with havoc and mayhem.

Youth is so precious.

When the cadets awoke, they were clear-eyed and ready to wreak havoc and mayhem of their own.

Today, however, they did not seem as sharp as usual. Even the calico was slouching her way through Hammer Claw. So I stopped the practice and berated her as weak and stupid, as all good teachers must do when they see their students failing.

That done, I addressed the three of them.

"Do you not want to become great warriors? Do you want to become *this*?" I pointed to Flabby Tabby, who was inhaling kibble six pellets at a time.

"Mrow?" he said, lifting his head.

"This! This pathetic excuse of a feline is your fate. Your only escape is to do precisely what I demand!"

At that moment, my inspirational speech was interrupted by a voice.

We were not alone!

"A lord stood before a vast assembly of soldiers.
Gazing upon them, he judged them inferior.
But he stood in a hall of mirrors,
For the only one substandard was himself."

Ffangg! He was *here*! In the bunker!

"I do love the ancient poets," he said, coming out from under the stairs. "So much *wisdom* in their verses."

"Stop with your nonsense!" I demanded. "How did
you infiltrate my war room?!"

Ffangg licked his paw calmly. "True warriors
guard their secrets like glittering jewels." He glanced
around the basement. "So this is the place where the
once-mighty warlord has chosen to retire. A dank
underground bunker that smells"—and here he raised
his nose and sniffed—"like the stinking breath of furless
ogres."

My tail puffed in indignation. "It is not dank, and it smells like the pine-scented sand of my litter."

Ffangg shook his head. "It is even worse than I thought."

"*What's* worse?"

"You!" he said. "You have become one of *them*."

"Nonsense!" I said, snarling.

"Look at you," he said with pretend pity. "You have grown fat and weak—you have forgotten how to forage off the land, how to steal from your enemies. You are petted and coddled. You have become . . . an *Earth cat*."

An **Earth cat**? This was the one insult I could not bear! I lunged at the traitor, but he dodged my attack. He leaped to the windowsill and gazed down at me mockingly.

"The old Wyss-Kuzz would never have missed," he said. Then he turned his attention to the kittens. "I daresay you have already learned all that this one has to teach you. Besides, I can offer you more than this dismal cavern. I have an entire citadel requisitioned for my purposes. A place *free* of ogres." He smiled slyly. "Perhaps, young warriors, you would like to visit."

The grays looked to their sister for guidance, while the calico in turn looked to Ffangg, and then to me. I had to display my power.

"Enough!" I shouted. "You have insulted me in my own bunker, in front of my troops! For these transgressions and others, I challenge you to . . . the Duel of the Branch!"

Ffangg smiled his smug, wide-whiskered grin and purred. "Oh, Wyss-Kuzz," he said, "I *happily* accept."

CHAPTER 29

Less than two weeks had passed, and Cameron had already made groupies of half the kids at school. Brody was the worst. For days, he'd been following Cam around like some kind of paparazzo, snapping pictures on his phone while Cam signed this or that kid's copy of Americaman.

What was even more sickening, though, was that Cameron had taken Scorpion and Newt's stupid Ro-butt and was in the process of turning it into something that looked like it could fly to Mars.

I wanted to win the robot competition so badly I could taste it, and Cam was going to ruin that, too!

"What do you think their drone's gonna *do*?" Steve said, unable to keep from staring at them.

"Who cares?" Cedar said. "We have to get the Aqua-

Bot's water dispensers working by tomorrow for the big demo or Miss Natasha will tear us apart."

"We need more time," Steve said.

We decided we would take the Aqua-Bot back to my house to work on it when the lab closed.

"Hey! Maybe we should ask *Cameron* to help us," Steve said.

"No!" I shouted, and Cedar gave me a funny look. "I just . . . want to work on it with you guys," I added.

Steve shrugged. "Fine, but he seems to know a lot about robots. And he *is* cool. Look," he said, reaching into his book bag and pulling out a stack of books. "He signed my *entire* series of Americaman."

"Why does everyone love Americaman so much, anyway?" Cedar said. She picked up *Americaman #4* with scorn. "Look at this one! *Attack of the Alien Hamsters*! Like aliens look like *pets*."

"Actually . . . ," I said.

"Yeah, we know, Raj," Steve said, rolling his eyes. "It's like you told us at camp. Your cat's an ALIEN!"

"Ugh, I'm sorry I mentioned it," Cedar said. "Look, we have to focus on the Aqua-Bot. There's still a whole list of stuff to fix."

"But the fart sounds are perfect now," Steve pointed out.

So we had *that* much going for us.

CHAPTER 30

The kitten commandos trotted after me in the glorious sunset of the cool evening, their tails like tiny flags of victory. And somewhere behind them, no doubt, lumbered Flabby Tabby and the dim-witted Ginger. Soon they would *all* witness Ffangg's final Downfall.

Ah, the Downfall! The fate of he who loses the Duel of the Branch.

The rules for the Duel of the Branch were scratched in stone in the year 28-962-D, and for millennia they had been held sacred by all cats. This ritualistic battle was an ancient and honorable means to settle an argument—and a way to bring an enemy to ruin and humiliation.

Purr.

We arrived at Ffangg's fortress. To give the

traitor his due, it did indeed warrant the term *citadel*. It was enormous, and it had a FOR SALE sign erected upon its front lawn. (Another curiosity of Human life: They considered *themselves* to be the owners of their possessions. Didn't they realize that all property belonged to their supreme warlord? But I digress.)

I called the traitor out to battle.

He was already in the yard, waiting for me in the shade of a rosebush. He was eating something. "The small rodents of this planet are as slow and stupid as its cats," Ffangg mused. "Catching my dinner was no effort at all."

My enemy finished slurping up the innards of whatever creature he had captured, and crunched its bones between his teeth.

It was a nice touch.

"I am not here to make conversation," I declared. "I am here to *fight*."

Ffangg bowed his head. "And with great pleasure shall I defeat you."

We walked to the rear of the citadel, where a tall tree grew. As the ancient protocols demanded, we circled its base, scratched at its trunk, and chanted the Oath of the Duel:

"Two climb up!
One will stay! One will fall!
He who remains
Is the leader of us all!"

The kittens watched intently. I trusted they would learn something from my inevitable victory. Ginger, too, was paying close attention, but Flabby had already fallen asleep.

With a final flick of our tails, we ascended the tree. The rules were simple: Whoever knocked the other from the branch claimed victory. No claws were allowed, and each contestant could use only one paw at a time to bat his foe.

I turned to Ffangg. "Are you ready, traitor?"

He answered with three quick swipes of his left paw.

I easily dodged his blows. "Can't even wait for the customary count of two, Ffangg?"

"Strike fast, strike first!" Ffangg crowed.

I cuffed him on his cheek as an answer to his insolence. Then I reached with my other paw to strike at his shoulder. I ducked his next swing, and at the same time used my right hind leg as a surprise cudgel, jackhammering him with a blurred series of blows.

"Mrow mrow MROW!" Ginger cheered me on. The boys were cheering for me as well, but the calico had no loyalty. She only applauded violence.

As Ffangg tried to defend himself against my furious flurry, I surprised him with a fast left paw to the shoulder. I caught him! He wobbled. He was on the cusp of falling!

I went for the **death blow**!

And . . .

CHAPTER 31

Cedar and Steve worked with me on the Aqua-Bot until they had to go home for dinner. I was still cleaning up when the doorbell rang. As much as I wanted it to be the other space kitty, it was probably just Steve. He was always forgetting stuff.

But it wasn't Steve. It was *Cameron*.

I didn't even have time to open my mouth before he started talking.

"I can't believe we moved here," Cam said, brushing past me into the house. "I mean, how could we leave Brooklyn for *this*?"

It was like he was already in the middle of a conversation. Which was kind of appropriate, because the only conversation Cam found interesting these days was with himself.

"The kids here, they follow me around like puppies! They think I'm so cool because I'm from New York and my mom writes Americaman. And I'm like, no, I'm not *that* cool."

"Well—"

"But they don't believe me. They're like, no, you really are *that cool.*"

"Um, yeah—"

Cam sighed. "It's hard when *everyone* wants to be your friend. How do you know who to pick?"

It sounded like a question, but Cameron wasn't looking for me to answer. He wouldn't even let me finish a sentence.

"But do I really want to be friends with *any* of these dorks? They won't leave me alone. They even follow me into the bathroom! 'Hey, Cameron, is Americaman going to defeat the Space Squids?' 'Hey, Cameron, will your mom put *me* in a comic?'"

As hard as it was to believe, Cam had gotten to be even more of a bigheaded jerk than before. He started going on about how there was an Americaman movie in production, and Americaman this, and Americaman that, and I just couldn't take it anymore!

"Maybe if you quit talking about Americaman for five seconds, they *would* leave you alone," I blurted out.

Cameron turned to me, his face full of shock and disgust. "I knew it! You're jealous!"

"I am not jealous."

"Oh, yeah?" he said with a sneer. "Then how come you told all the kids around here that you were my friend just so you would be popular?"

I could feel myself shrink.

"And I guess you told everybody we're not best friends anymore," I said. "To humiliate me."

"Why would I want to humiliate you?" Cameron asked. "I think it's cute the way you idolize me. I mean, it's pathetic, but I totally don't mind."

"I do *not* idolize you! You were ten times dorkier than me before your mom got famous! And why would I idolize someone who acts like a big JERK all the time?"

Cameron glared at me. "Yeah, go ahead and put me down. I'm cool and you're not. Your dad is a *dentist*, and my mom is the GREATEST COMIC BOOK WRITER IN THE WORLD!"

That was it! He couldn't drag my *dad* into this!

"Yeah, well, I have excellent oral hygiene, and my mom is your dad's *boss*!" I said. "And just because your **mom** does something awesome, it doesn't make **you** awesome! Not that it's even that awesome anymore. Americaman was WAY BETTER when it was a web comic!"

I had just crossed a line and I knew it. But so had he!

Cam looked like Starsey Stripes when he was just about to deliver a star-spangled roundhouse. But instead, he turned to leave.

"You'll be sorry for what you said, Banerjee," Cameron said. "I'm going to **get** you for this!"

He slammed the door so hard the windowpanes rattled.

CHAPTER 32

The force of the would-be death blow unbalanced me. I wobbled, trying desperately to keep my clawhold, but I had left myself too exposed.

All Ffangg had to do was reach out his paw . . . and push.

Suddenly I was falling through the air. Wind rushed through my fur as I plunged downward.

This could not be happening! This was a nightmare! I was in such a state of shock, I failed to execute the proper in-flight rotation before I hit the ground.

And so I landed—not on all fours—but on my **back**.

Oof!

Ffangg jumped gracefully down from the tree. I didn't need to see his face to know the look of his gloating.

"I would say you gave it a good try, Wyss-Kuzz,"
he said, "but you did not." He paused to draw out his
triumph. "You *know* what comes next, don't you," he said.

I did.

It was written that he who suffers the Downfall
must . . . must . . .

Oh, I could not bear to even think about it!

"Behold, young warriors, what comes to he who
falls and fails." Ffangg bowed his head. "Go ahead, oh
great warrior. *Lick.*"

For this was written in the ancient rules: The loser
of the Duel of the Branch must groom the head of the
winner.

Though I would rather rip out my own tongue than
place it against my enemy's fur, to fail to do so would
bring eternal shame.

So I did it.

I licked Ffangg's forehead.

"Oh, that's nice! Don't forget behind the ears,
Klawdie," Ffangg said.

When it was finally over, I hacked up seven hairballs.

"I almost feel sorry for him," Ffangg said, turning to
the kittens. "You could hardly guess it, but Wyss-Kuzz
was great once. *Once*, but no more!"

"Don't listen to him, cadets! I slipped—it proves

nothing!" I said. "Let us return to the bunker."

The gray boys turned to their sister. She looked to me, then to Ffangg, and then she went over and rubbed against *him*.

Betrayed—again!

"Do not feel bad, old friend," Ffangg purred. "You always believe yourself to be a victim of treason, but someday you will realize that it is merely the way of the cat to follow the strong and despise the weak."

My rage burned like a thousand supernovas, as did my shame. I would have my revenge—on ALL of them.

CHAPTER 33

Dinner was dismal. Between my fight with Cam and the big robot demo coming up, I was in no mood to talk. Luckily, my parents spent the entire meal arguing over who had forgotten to plug in Mom's new electric car, so I didn't have to.

When Klawde finally came home, well after dark, I went downstairs and told him about what had happened with Cam. The amazing thing was that Klawde was actually listening this time. Not only that, he was totally sympathetic.

"The foes of the past should not be allowed to ruin the present! Something must be done to enemies such as this! Their insults cannot be allowed to stand without retribution!"

"Max and Brody both like Cam better than me now,"

I said. "I think even *Steve* might."

"The ungrateful mob! They are never loyal! Lowly peons always follow those perceived to be more powerful! They are deserters! Turncoats! Treacherous fools!"

I had never seen Klawde like this! Spitting and hissing and seething with fury.

Well, I actually *had* seen Klawde like this. A lot. Just never on my behalf. It made me feel good that he cared so much.

"The penalties must be severe! Mortifying and unmerciful!" Klawde went on. "String all the traitors up by their claws, I say!"

Claws?

"You mean fingernails," I said.

"What?" Klawde said.

"The traitors and peons and all that—they don't have claws," I said.

Then he looked at me like I was the stupidest creature in the universe. "Of course they have claws!" he said.

"Wait—who are you talking about?" I said.

"The kittens, you furless idiot! And Ffangg!"

Sigh. "So you *don't* actually care about my problems," I said.

He again gave me the look. "What kind of question is that?" he said. "Of course I don't."

CHAPTER 34

Honestly! Didn't the ogre know me by now?

Why would I care about his "friendships"? I was talking about my army! Who had deserted me and chosen to follow my greatest enemy—the one who had ruined me on Lyttyrboks! And now he was doing it all over again on Earth!

He must be **stopped**!

"Hey," the boy-Human said, looking around the bunker. "Where are the kittens, anyway?"

HISSSSSSSSSSSSSSSSSSSSSSSSS!

"Ouch!" the ogre said, grabbing at his leg. His hideous bare skin now bore four perfectly parallel scratch lines. But even the sight of them couldn't bring me pleasure.

(Well, *fleeting* pleasure.)

"What's wrong with you, Klawde? What did you do *that* for?"

So I told the boy-ogre everything. Even about . . . the grooming.

Hack! Hack! Reliving the experience brought up another hairball.

"I'm sorry Ffangg stole your friends," Raj said.

"They are not my *friends*! They are my soldiers!" I spat at him. "But I will make them pay! All of them! Ffangg and those three little turncoats! I will make them wish they'd never been born to the flea-ridden she-cat who bore them!"

"Why don't you win the kittens back to your side?" the boy-Human said, still rubbing his wounded leg. "Just make Ffangg look worse than he made *you* look, and the kittens will leave him as quickly as they left you."

Win them back rather than destroy them? By the eighty-seven moons, I did believe the Human was on to something. Usually he was so disappointing. But the more I thought about it, the better it sounded.

As the saying goes, *Out of the mouths of complete idiots . . .*

CHAPTER 35

As Cedar, Steve, and I—and the Aqua-Bot!—came walking and rolling up to school the next morning, all the kids stopped to look.

"Cool!"

"No way!"

"Who built that?"

I was feeling better than I had in a while.

Until, that is, I heard a low whirring sound—and a gasp from Steve. I turned around and saw Cameron and Scorpion and Newt's drone, lights flashing, swooping and diving over the parking lot. All the kids who'd been admiring the Aqua-Bot immediately ran over to get a closer look at the drone.

In robotics, it was the exact same thing—the whole class oohing and aahing from the moment Miss

Natasha picked Cam's team to go first. When they fired up their robot, the drone buzzed about the room as Cam described what it did.

"This is Dr. Drone," he said. "A flying first-aid kit. It has Band-Aids, an EpiPen, and an inhaler for kids with asthma."

"Wow, that *is* cool," Steve said admiringly.

"And in case of an emergency . . ."

Cam turned on the siren, which sounded like an ambulance. The other kids all cheered and clapped—they freaking loved it. Newt and Scorpion high-fived each other while Cam just stood there, looking super smug, like he already knew he was the winner.

Miss Natasha, though, wasn't quite as impressed. "It's a very nice concept," she said. "However, it's not that practical in our school."

Cam looked surprised, and Scorpion looked shocked. "But it FLIES!" he said.

Miss Natasha pointed out that kids with asthma already carried inhalers, while those with allergies kept EpiPens in their backpacks. And did Band-Aids really need to arrive through the air? A student could walk to the school nurse quicker than they could summon a drone. "And besides," Miss Natasha said, "what part of your project uses recycled parts?"

"But it FLIES!" Scorpion said again.

Cameron, meanwhile, just silently seethed.

Next we watched demonstrations by a robot that dusted shelves and another that brushed teeth—neither of which worked very well. They were followed by a robot that short-circuited before we even found out what the heck its purpose was.

Finally, it was our turn.

I took a deep breath as Cedar worked the controller and made our robot come to life. "Meet the Aqua-Bot!" I said, just like we had scripted.

"Water for sale! Only a nickel!" it chirped. *"Get it FLAT . . . or get it FIZZY!"*

"Check it out!" Steve said. He pressed each of the fizzy buttons, and the Aqua-Bot made louder and louder fart sounds.

Everyone laughed. Even Scorpion found it funny.

Only Cam sat stone-faced.

"It's cheaper than vending machines," Cedar said, "and it doesn't waste plastic. It'll pour water into your own reusable container—or right into your mouth."

Steve crouched down in front of the Aqua-Bot. A stream of water shot right down his throat.

He drank for a minute and then sat up grinning. "Delicious!" he said.

"All proceeds will be sent to Water for Folks," I said, "an international organization that works to get fresh, clean water to those who need it."

The other students politely clapped, and everyone looked to see what Miss Natasha would say. She hadn't been particularly pleased with *anyone's* project.

But now she smiled.

She said that she was super impressed by our creative reuse of old parts. But even more, she liked how the Aqua-Bot served a true need, both in terms of health and the environment. The fact that we were raising money for a worthy cause made it even *more* fantastic.

"I would like the Aqua-Bot to represent our robotics class at this year's Wormy Apple Harvest Festival next weekend," she said. "But as a final demonstration, you'll showcase the Aqua-Bot alongside all the other exhibitors at the school assembly on Monday."

We won! We actually *won*! It was amazing. The icing on the cake was Cam's face. My former friend looked like *he* was on the verge of short-circuiting.

CHAPTER 36

All day, I stewed in the bilious juices of my fury. I must have my revenge! But how? By what means?

As my massive feline brain analyzed all the possible stratagems, the boy-Human arrived home. I hissed at him to leave me alone, as I needed privacy for my scheming. His pestering, however, was relentless.

"But, Klawde, don't you understand? Our robot **won**! On Monday I get to show it off to the whole school!" He was practically jumping up and down with excitement. It was most unseemly.

"And I care *why*?"

The ogre emitted a groan. "I've been working on the Aqua-Bot for weeks and you still don't even know what it does! You have to come see it!"

To finally put the matter to rest—and get him to leave

me alone—I agreed to look at his school project. I could only imagine how pathetic and worthless it would be.

I yawned as the boy fiddled with a primitive controller for the robot, which I had seen in the garage but assumed to be a pile of what the ogres called "recycling."

"Hurry it up, Human," I said. "I have work to do. Revenge doesn't plan itself."

The young ogre smiled and said, "Here we go, Klawde!"

"Water for sale! Only a nickel!"

The robot spoke! It moved! And with a sound like the gaseous blast of a Hexian space troll, it emitted a stream of that most horrible Earth substance—WATER!

My back arched in self-protection, and the fur along my spine stood on end. This robot was the most nefarious weapon I had ever laid eyes upon! *This* was what he had been making in school? My respect for Raj increased exponentially.

I also couldn't believe my luck. For days I had been seeking the instrument of my revenge, and lo and behold, here it was in my own fortress.

Immediately, I asked the ogre many questions about this "Aqua-Bot." Somehow he failed to see it as a weapon—he envisioned his creation as something "helpful to humanity." Like Humanity needed to be helped! Ha! Imprisoned and enslaved, yes. Helped? Definitely not.

After the boy-ogre had gone to sleep and the parent-ogres had fallen into their nocturnal trance of the screen, I reentered the garage to give the fiendish device a more thorough inspection. The design was simplistic—after all, it *was* Human—but it presented many possibilities for improvement.

I napped only seventeen times that next day, so consumed was I in scheming and planning. And on the following night, I executed my changes to the evil Aqua-Bot.

I redirected the liquid-spraying guns to a more effective angle: straight ahead, the better to aim at one's foes. To increase the power and range of each stream, I increased the gas compression charges to their maximum force.

When I was finished, I gazed upon it in awe and admiration.

It was BRILLIANT!

CHAPTER 37

"I still think fire is a weird decoration for a *water* robot," Cedar said.

I ignored her as I added the last bit of orange to the flames I was painting on the side of the Aqua-Bot.

"Yeah, water totally puts out fire, Raj," Steve said. "But then again, fire can boil water and turn it to steam! So it's like . . . what's the word? Oh, yeah. *Confusing.*"

"No, it's not confusing," Cedar said, "it's just weird."

"Weird? Are you guys kidding me? I think it's AWESOME!"

It was my dad, coming into the garage even though I'd begged him not to.

"*Wicked* awesome." He stood there grinning at us.

"Did you need something, Dad?" I asked.

"Oh, yeah! I came to tell you that the pizza's here!"

"Thanks, Dr. B.," Cedar said.

"PIZZZZZZZA!" Steve yelled like it was some kind of war cry as he sprinted out of the room.

Dad stayed behind with me, gazing at the Aqua-Bot. "Super, *super* awesome! I can't believe you designed this! You're so cool, I need to put on a jacket!" He pretended to shiver as he clapped me on the back.

"Um, yeah, right," I muttered.

Dad said he was going to go eat some pizza, and I told him I needed a few more minutes to finish the flames. Which I didn't—I just wanted to stand back and admire them.

They **did** look awesome. Everyone was going to *love* the Aqua-Bot at the school assembly tomorrow.

But something made me do a double take. Was the angle of the water pistols correct? Did the hose setup look, I don't know, a little different? The assembly was first thing tomorrow, and I didn't want anything to be off.

"Raj!" Cedar yelled from the kitchen. "Steve's plowing through the pepperoni slices like the Tasmanian Devil, and I can only guard the veggie pizza for so long!"

"All right, all right, I'm coming!" I hollered back.

I was being crazy. How could anything be wrong with the Aqua-Bot? We'd worked so hard on the thing. It was *perfect*.

CHAPTER 38

As soon as the Humans retired for the evening,
I seized the controller and activated the Aqua-Bot.
Quickly silencing its vocal component, I directed the evil
robot out the side entrance of the garage. Then I climbed
atop the mechanical monster and pointed it in the
direction of my enemy. Passing the house of the Flabby
Tabby, I saw the face of his girl-Human in the window.
Her mouth fell open in awe.

That's right! Your disgusting slob of a cat can't do this!

If only this robot weren't so slow.

When finally I arrived at Ffangg's citadel, I put the
next phase of my scheme into action.

"Ffangg!" I called out. "I have come to bury this
pointless feud of ours! Let us agree to live out our exiles
in peace. To forget what has transpired in the past. To—"

I had to stop there. I couldn't continue such lies without coughing up another hairball.

Ffangg appeared in an upper window, suspicion in his eyes. The kittens peeked over his shoulder. "So, the mighty warlord has finally come to his senses, eh? Then why is it that my whiskers detect the quickened pulse of a LIAR?"

"Come see for yourself my sincerity!" I said.

And to my surprise, the treasonous general leaped out the window and landed nimbly on the lawn. The gray kittens followed him, tumbling and sliding down the porch roof. The calico, however, hung back. Her instincts were most keen!

"What is this pitiful plastic contraption?" Ffangg said, his suspicion now replaced by mocking good cheer. "Have you become so feeble and Earthlike that you require a machine to move you from place to place?"

The sound of his purr might have enraged me, but I

purred back, knowing I had the upper paw.

"Pitiful?" I said. "Oh, I think you might change your opinion on that."

"I highly doubt it. Everything I see on this planet is pitiful," Ffangg said. "Most especially *you*."

"What was that you once said to me, Ffangg?" I asked. "Something about how it is better to be quick with the claw than fast with the tongue?"

Before he could answer, I pressed a button and the water pistols **fired**!

Ffangg was instantly soaked to the skin!

The yowl of his humiliation echoed through the night, and the traitor retreated up a tree, drenched and panting. I could see his heart beating through his fur. His eyes were wide with terror!

Purrrr!

"No witty ripostes now, eh, General?" I called. "Shame, thy name is Ffangg!"

The boy-kittens looked to their sister, hoping she could help them decipher this sudden turn of fortune. Ffangg, sensing how precarious his power base had become, moved to descend the tree. A flurry of laser-like liquid blasts unleashed in his direction, however, sent him scurrying right back up.

When he was soaked and shivering to my satisfaction, I turned the robot back toward my fortress.

"Commandos!" I called. "It is time to leave!"

Ffangg could do nothing but watch as the calico followed my orders, leaping atop the Aqua-Bot and yowling for her brethren to follow. My young protégé was becoming quite the leader in her own right.

Her spirit would need crushing soon. But that was for another day—tonight I would celebrate my triumph!

CHAPTER 39

On Monday morning, the whole school gathered in the gym, and Principal Brownepoint motioned for us all to be quiet. "It's time for our sneak preview of the Wormy Apple Harvest Fest," he said, "which is when we get to show the entire Elba community our Fightin' Bookworm *pride*!"

First the Street Performer Intensive showed off their juggling skills (pretty cool). Then the Tuba Club played a Sousa march (pretty uncool), and the fencing team demonstrated various sword-fighting techniques (less cool than it sounds). After the choir sang a Beatles medley, it was finally time for robotics.

Cedar, Steve, and I brought out the Aqua-Bot, which started and stopped with perfect smoothness.

"Water for sale! Only a nickel! Get it flat or get it fizzy!"

"Do we have a volunteer?" I asked.

Max popped up and put a nickel into the robot's coin slot. He held a cup under the squirt gun spigot, but instead of immediately dispensing water, it swiveled upward and pointed right at Max's nose. Meanwhile, the fizzy fart sounds were ripping through the room like sonic explosions. What was going on? Before I could even guess, the Aqua-Bot shot a stream of mega-fizzy water right into Max's face!

"Hey, quit it!" the poor kid cried.

But the Aqua-Bot did *not* quit it. It spun around toward the crowd and fired another jet of water. Two supercharged streams drenched the kids in the front row of the bleachers.

"*Do I detect . . . THIRST?*" the Aqua-Bot said, shooting another carbonated laser at a bunch of eighth-graders.

I was hitting every button on the controller, but

the Aqua-Bot wasn't responding! It shot the coffee out of Miss Natasha's hand, and next it sprayed water at *Principal Brownepoint,* nailing him right in the crotch of his pants. It looked like he'd peed himself!

Every student in the school was laughing now. Except the three of us who had created the Aqua-Bot.

And Cameron. The expression on his face reminded

me of how Klawde looked when he mangled a piece of furniture. Like he was *pleased with himself*.

As for the Aqua-Bot, it was still spraying, and a giant puddle of water had begun spreading across the gym floor. I was frozen in panic.

Thankfully, Cedar was not. She darted forward and managed to yank the battery pack out of the back of the Aqua-Bot. It immediately stopped, its water pistols slowly tilting toward the floor.

"Aww!" the other kids in the gym hollered. Then they started to cheer.

How had this *happened*? The Aqua-Bot was working perfectly the last time we used it! And it wasn't even like it was malfunctioning—it was as if it had been *programmed* to fire like that.

Someone must have sabotaged the Aqua-Bot. But who? It had to be someone who knew a lot about robotics. And someone who wanted to hurt our group.

Or hurt me.

I looked again at Cam, still grinning. He looked right back at me, and he winked.

CHAPTER 40

When the boy-Human returned from school, he related a day of disaster and chaos. Naturally this was more interesting than his usual blather, and I relished my role in the fiasco.

It was a role, however, that I tactfully—and tactically—decided to keep to myself. The ogre believed that his *enemy* had sabotaged his creation! I allowed him to think this, not only because it concealed my guilt in the affair, but also because it might finally spur the feckless Human to action.

"What you must do is clear," I said. "You and your comrades must band together and make this Cameron rue the day he was born!"

"We humans don't go around avenging ourselves all the time, Klawde," the ogre said. "We'd get in trouble."

"Listen, hairless one. There are many ways to defeat an enemy. You do not need to harm him. You must simply humiliate him."

"I don't know . . ."

"Show some courage, ogre! By humiliating Ffangg I have turned the tables back in my favor!"

"Wait, you did? How?"

"How is not the point, ogre! The fact is, I did it, and now my troops have returned to me!"

"You mean the kittens are here again?" the Human said excitedly.

He hurried to the box in which my commandos were quietly resting.

"Hey, little guys!"

The calico growled at him, and the ogre shrank back in apprehension. I could hardly blame him. The she-cat had grown considerably in the last week and was ever more imposing. She spit in his direction and took a leaping swipe at him, claws out.

"Okay, I guess I'll pet you later," the ogre said. "Or never."

"As the great Lord Feelyne said, *It is better to shatter a reputation than to shatter a sword,*" I said. "Shame this fellow ogre well enough and he will never bother you again. If you instead allow *yourself* to be shamed, the universe will never stop humiliating you."

The Human digested the obvious wisdom of my words. Perhaps one day he would even act upon them.

That night, I went to nap happy. Many times I awoke and napped again, blissfully reliving my victory. But sometime in the wee hours of dawn, I awoke in the bunker, shivering. I felt a wicked, hateful chill.

I turned to look at my tail. It was something I often did, considering its magnificence.

And it was at this moment that I saw the greatest horror of my life.

CHAPTER 41

On Tuesday, we got the news we probably should've been expecting: The Aqua-Bot would NOT be representing the robotics class at Harvest Fest. Instead, it would be Dr. Drone. Cameron's face practically split in two, he was smiling so wide, and he and Newt and Scorpion all high-fived each other.

Miss Natasha said she didn't want to make the switch, but Principal Brownepoint demanded it. "Everyone knows that water and robots don't mix," he'd said. "It's unnatural!"

"He's just mad the Aqua-Bot made it look like he'd peed his pants," Cedar said.

"We have to get Cam back for this," I said to her and Steve as we walked home from school together.

"He's so cool, though," Steve said. "I can't believe

he'd sabotage our project. That would just be evil."

"It's obvious he did it," I said. "He couldn't stand that we built a better robot than his team did, and he's out to get me because of the fight we had."

"But revenge?" Cedar said. "I mean, I'm all for it, but it doesn't seem very like you, Raj."

And it wasn't. But I had decided that Klawde was right—I had to stand up for myself. But I couldn't tell them that I was taking advice from a feline space alien, so I just shrugged.

"Well, whatever," Cedar said. "I'm in. Let's take Dr. Drone and turn him back into the Butt-bot. Wedgies for all!"

"I don't want to humiliate *everyone*—not even Scorpion and Newt," I said. "Just Cameron."

"We could smash his drone," Steve said. "I'm good at breaking stuff."

But I had a different idea. "You know how everybody

thinks the siren recording is so cool? What if we reprogram the drone's recorder so it plays *this*?" I stuck my hand in my armpit and made a super-loud farting noise.

Steve immediately started doing it, too. "That's an *awesome* idea," he said.

Cedar rolled her eyes. "It's actually totally lame," she said. "But whatever. It's better than just standing around doing nothing."

"All right then, it's decided," I said. "Tomorrow, we go over to Cameron's house and make the switch."

"But how do we get *in* there?" Cedar said. "He's going to be suspicious if we all show up at his door and are like, *Hey, we'd like to play with your robot.*"

I had an idea for that. But Cedar was *not* going to like it.

CHAPTER 42

My tail! My beautiful—majestic—*magnificent* tail!

It had been . . .

SHAVED!

How could this have happened? It was impossible to believe. The humiliation! I had gone from victor to vanquished in a matter of hours!

The calico woke and crept toward me, her brothers following. I hissed at them. "Halt, cadets!" I cried.

I backed into the corner so they could not see my shame. "Go back to nap," I commanded.

The boys obeyed, but their sister stood her ground and cocked her head, sensing something amiss.

Then a voice rang out from the shadows. "And now we see who has sunk the lowest of all!"

Ffangg! The traitorous tail-shaver was still in my bunker! I wanted nothing more than to shred him to bits, but to come out of the corner would expose my naked tail. I could not allow the kittens to see what Ffangg had done. "Come over here so I can scratch out your eyeballs!"

But Ffangg ignored me. "Sally forth and investigate,

young warriors," he said to the kittens. "See the shame of your so-called leader! Behold his backside! Could a real leader allow an enemy to sneak into his fortress at night and *shave his tail*? No, the true warlord sleeps with one eye open! Only a cat whose senses are blunt and whose mind is soft could be humiliated so completely!"

Ffangg pushed a fluffy gray ball into the center of the room. The calico pounced on it and began to rip it with her back claws.

Ffangg's purr echoed against the bunker walls. "Behold, Klawde, how your soldier shreds the remains of your tail!"

Humiliation overwhelmed me. My mind raced for my next move, but what could I do? Nothing! I could only crouch there, with my tail underneath me, and pretend that nothing—*absolutely* nothing—was amiss.

CHAPTER 43

I'd spent half an hour explaining to Klawde how I was going to get back at Cam, and he hadn't said a single word. That wasn't exactly unusual, but this was a plan about *revenge*.

"It's your favorite subject!" I said.

Still nothing.

The *really* weird thing, however, was how he refused to come out from under my dad's La-Z-Boy. I asked him if something was wrong, and he didn't answer. Then I asked where the kittens had gone off to. Still nothing.

"Does it have something to do with Ffangg?"

Klawde hissed.

Well, at least I knew he was alive under there.

Finding out what his deal was would have to wait

for later, though, because right then the doorbell rang.

I ran upstairs and flung open the door. "Did you read it?" I asked Cedar, who was standing on the porch next to Steve.

She rolled her eyes, opened her book bag, and took out *Americaman #3: The Fiendish Plot of General Coup.* "It's basically the dumbest thing I've ever had the misfortune of looking at."

"She's insane," Steve said. "General Coup is Americaman's best villain!"

Cedar ignored him. "You'd better be quick in there, Raj, because if I have to fake this for too long, I'm going to barf," she said.

Cam seemed a little suspicious when he answered the door, but right away Cedar started gushing about the comic and asking him to autograph it. Then he let us right in.

He was home alone, and his house was practically a mansion. Somehow it looked like he and his family had lived there forever, whereas my house *still* had moving boxes everywhere.

"I love this part here," Cedar said, flipping through the comic. "And *this* part is hilarious."

I could tell she was just randomly pointing at pages, but she was a good actor. Steve didn't need to act, obviously, because he did think Americaman was the greatest thing ever.

"*So* hilarious!" he repeated.

Cam soaked it all up. Then he started talking about how there was going to be an Americaman movie, and that the producers were coming up from L.A. to take his family out to a big fancy dinner.

While Cam went on and on about how awesome the movie was going to be, I excused myself to the bathroom. Then I went looking for the drone.

I found it on their sunporch, which was stuffed full of Americaman merchandise—Americaman posters,

Americaman action figures, and even real-life models of Americaman's throwing stars. I went over to the drone and popped open its hood. Inside was the same kind of programmable mini-recorder we'd used for the Aqua-Bot. My heart pounded as I scrolled through the menu options.

I just needed to record a hidden track and set it to start playing at noon on Saturday, when the demos at the Harvest Fest were scheduled to begin. Programming the recorder was easy. The next part was not.

I hiked up my shirt, put my hand under my armpit, and flapped my elbow up and down like a chicken. But I couldn't make the fart noise! No matter how hard I tried, it just sounded like Miss Emmy Jo's miniature horse huffing as he jumped a tiny barrel.

"*What* is taking you so long?"

It was Steve.

"I'm too nervous—I can't do the noise!"

"Allow me," Steve said, sticking his hand up his shirt. And then he let it rip.

Steve's underarm flatulence was truly unparalleled.

Then the door swung open, and Cameron stood there glaring at us. "Are you guys FARTING in the Americaman room?" he asked.

"Sorry," I said, "Steve here has gastrointestinal issues."

Steve rubbed his stomach. "Yeah, and I had a really big bean burrito for lunch."

Cam was just about to say something when Cedar came in. "Wowwwww, a whole Americaman room! This is amazing," she said. She was laying it on pretty thick, but it worked. We got out of there without him suspecting a thing. And we barely made it a block before we burst out laughing.

CHAPTER 44

The most disturbing thing about my encounter with the boy-Human came after he left: I found myself *missing* him.

HOW COULD THIS BE?

I crawled out from underneath the father-Human's padded chair, but it would have been better had I not, because it was then that I came face-to-face with . . .

Myself.

Across the room hung one of the Humans' primitive reflection-makers, and in it I saw my shorn tail in all its bare monstrosity. Now I understood why the ogres wore clothing—to hide such hideousness!

Lying on the ground was one of the boy-Human's foot coverings. Bulky though it was, this "sock" was roughly the size of a tail.

With some effort, I managed to pull it on.

It looked **horrid**.

Although it was an improvement over bare skin, it filled me with deeper shame.

Turning away from the awful image of myself, I crept across the room to where the kittens used to sleep. Then I peered under the couch where the Flabby Tabby used to hide. Oh, that silly Flabby!

One of his catnip toys lay on the carpet. I sniffed. Such a glorious *smell*! I had forgotten how enchanting its aroma was. I could imagine myself winning wars again when I smelled such a smell as this. I saw myself leading troops to battle! Destroying Ffangg! And—oh, glory of glories!—I could see Flooffee-Fyr arriving here to take me home to Lyttyrboks. *Finally! Finally you have come, Flooffee!*

The dreams were so vivid, they seemed utterly real.

Was I napping? Was I awake? I could no longer tell.

Suddenly, I felt an overwhelming, all-consuming **hunger**. I pounced on the kibble the boy-ogre had left for me. I didn't even chew the rocklike pellets, I swallowed them whole. Next I turned my attention to the canned food, which had grown hard and crusty, and yet which I devoured as if it were the hearts of my enemies!

I ate so much that my stomach hurt and I had to lie on my back.

Then I dreamed more glorious dreams. I was on Lyttyrboks again, ruling with an iron paw, making my enemies cower and beg for mercy. I never wanted to wake up.

CHAPTER 45

"Well, shucks, Fightin' Eel Worms, I hope y'all are as excited as pigs in a peach orchard about the Wormy Apple Harvest Festival on Saturday! The fun starts at eleven, and the demonstrations start at noon sharp, but if I were you, I'd get there early. It's gonna be a rager!"

Miss Emmy Jo's words rang in my ears all day. The truth was, I *was* excited. I still wished the Aqua-Bot had gotten a second chance to impress everyone. But since there was no way to make that happen, I could look forward to the next best thing: watching Cameron's face when Dr. Drone's fart mix started playing.

All that worried me now was Klawde. He hadn't come up for his egg and butter breakfast for days, but he *had* taken to eating the kibble and canned tuna my dad left out for him. Klawde *hated* cat food. Something had to be wrong with him. And where the heck were the kittens? I missed them, even the scary calico.

After school, I went straight home to talk to him.

He was still under the La-Z-Boy. And the basement smelled awful.

"Klawde," I said. "Have you been farting?"

There was no answer for a moment. Then he said a word I never thought I'd hear him say:

"Sorry."

Now I was **really** worried!

"Klawde, what's wrong?" I said. "Dad wants to call the vet, you know. It's been so long since you scratched him that all his wounds are healed. His hands look naked without the Band-Aids!"

"I'm not sick," Klawde said. "And even if I was, I wouldn't let you take me to one of your Human witch doctors."

"Unless you come out right now and tell me what's

wrong, we *are* going to the vet," I said.

"Fine," he sighed.

Klawde being obedient? What was going *on*?

"I don't even care anymore who bears witness to my disgrace," he said. "Just buy me new catnip mice and leave me extra kibble rations."

Then Klawde crawled out from underneath the chair. My first thought was, *Well, he definitely wasn't starving under there.*

And my second thought was, "Why are you wearing one of my socks on your tail?"

"Sock?" he said. "What sock? That's how my tail has always looked."

"Come on, Klawde, quit messing around," I said, and reached down to pull off the sock.

Oh . . . my . . . *wow*.

179

CHAPTER 46

I was exposed. But I didn't care anymore. I felt a void so deep and vast that not even reliving my best, most evil deeds could fill it.

All I wanted was to be left alone to sniff catnip, nap in the sun, and eat kibble. The kibble, it was true, had been making my stomach hurt, but I found that the release of gas from my backside gave me enough relief to eat more.

But the boy-ogre would not leave me alone, so I told him the entire wretched story of what had happened. He was furious at Ffangg on my behalf.

"He can't get away with this!"

"Oh, Raj!" I said. "Always rushing to my defense, no matter how much I point out your many flaws."

"You're using my *name*? You're being *considerate*?"

he said. "You're freaking me out, Klawde."

"I freak myself out," I said, and tried to slink back under the chair.

The boy-Human blocked me.

"Stop feeling sorry for yourself!" he said. "You're not the Flabby Tabby. You're the Evil Alien Warlord Cat! The greatest warmonger in the universe!"

"But my tail . . . ," I said.

"Your tail doesn't even look that bad!"

"Easy for you to say," I said. "You were born hideous."

I went to put the sock back on but the boy-ogre snatched it away.

"Klawde, you have to stop with all the kibble and catnip and hiding," he said. "You've let Ffangg get inside your head! You know those sayings you always quote? *Revenge is a dish best served as often as possible!* And, *Revenge is the best medicine!* Well, take your own advice.

I did, and now *my* enemy is going to be sorry he ever messed with me!"

The words stunned me. I had never heard my ogre so eloquent and convincing. Maybe what he said was true! After all, I **was** the greatest, most evil warlord the universe had ever known. Ffangg's treachery could not take that away!

And, relatively speaking, my tail *wasn't* so bad—I still had a thousand times more fur than the ogre did.

But what lifted my spirits was his talk of revenge. Just as solitude is the highest form of being on Lyttyrboks, so is revenge the supreme form of *action*. Remembering this broke the haze that had fogged my brain these past few days. Finally, I was thinking clearly again.

"Ogre, you may be stupid, you may be hideous, you may be one of the lowest life-forms I have ever come across, but this day you have spoken the **truth**!" I said. "And for this, I despise you somewhat less."

"That's my cat!" he said, smiling.

I hated when Humans did that.

In any case, what I needed was to rid the universe of Ffangg once and for all. And to achieve this end, I would challenge the traitorous general to one final contest.

I would reach back into ancient history to what had come before the Duel of the Branch, a form of fighting so brutal it had been banned since the year 493-A.

The Bout of the Box!

CHAPTER 47

"Hey, Ra-aj," called a voice. "Is Chad over at your house? He got out again."

It was Lindy, the annoying kid from across the street, and Chad was her cat—the one Klawde more accurately called the Flabby Tabby.

"Um, no, I don't think so."

"I've seen him in your yard a few times when he does get outside. Maybe he's friends with your kitty!"

"I seriously doubt it," I said.

I was hoping she wouldn't cross the street, but of course she did. She was clutching a copy of *Americaman #11: The Terrornado Blows*.

"Have you heard that the author of Americaman moved to Elba?" she asked. "And did you know she has a son? I saw him once on his skateboard. Can you believe that *they* would live *here*! They belong in some cool place, like Brooklyn!"

I didn't bother telling her that they actually *were* from Brooklyn, or that I knew Cam all too well. But I couldn't totally let Lindy's statement go.

"You know, I'm from Brooklyn," I said.

"Yeah, *right*!" she said, and laughed. "But don't feel bad, you're almost famous, too. My parents were reading about you in the newspaper. *AQUA-BOT ATROCITIES!*"

"Yeah, well—"

"I sure wish I could have been there to see that!" Lindy said, smiling at the thought. Then she scrunched up her nose. "The weird thing is that the Aqua-Bot looked like it was working fine the night before."

"What do you mean, the night before?" I asked. "*What* night before?"

"The night before it went all psycho at your school,

silly!" she said. "I saw it rolling down the sidewalk right before I went to bed."

"But—but," I stammered. "That's impossible!"

"That's what *I* thought. And then I figured out you had to be using a remote control." The smile popped back onto Lindy's face as she remembered something. "And it was so cute how you put your cat up on top of it! Chad would never be brave enough to ride a robot!"

Klawde? *Riding* the Aqua-Bot? The night before it . . .

Oh no!

I had made a **terrible** mistake!

CHAPTER 48

It had been many naptimes since I had left the
bunker, and many more since I had engaged in any sort
of physical conditioning.

As a result, I was somewhat larger than I was
accustomed to being. It seemed like a very long distance
indeed between my fortress and the street. So long, in
fact, that I was gasping for breath by the time I got to the
sidewalk.

This journey might take longer than anticipated.

The sun was still bright by the time I reached
Ffangg's citadel. My paws ached and my whiskers
drooped, but I rang out my challenge like the supreme
warrior I once had been—and would soon be again.

"Ffangg," I cried. "Come out of there and show your
two-faced face!"

My enemy emerged unhurriedly from his fortress. "What is this big, bellowing creature I see before me?" he said, whiskers twitching. "You almost look like an old friend of mine. Well, three or four of him."

"You know perfectly well who I am, traitor."

"Oh, Wyss-Kuzz, is that you? You really have . . . *grown*."

"Enough! I challenge you—"

"Wyss-Kuzz, we have been through this already," Ffangg said. "You lost, I won. It was all rather nice."

"That was a game for kittens," I declared. "Today I challenge you to the ultimate fight." I paused dramatically. *"The Bout of the Box."*

Ffangg's face! It looked like he'd just seen the ghost of King Si-uh-meez, whose spirit is known to appear to cats on their deathbed.

"You can't mean—"

"A FIGHT TO THE DEATH."

Ffangg glanced back at the kittens, who were watching avidly, and was forced to compose himself. "You really need not yell like that. My ears work perfectly well." He turned to the kittens. "You must forgive him. His senses have been dulled by excessive cat-to-ogre contact. It is extremely detrimental to feline health."

The calico looked at Ffangg with a fresh skepticism, and then to me with curiosity. If Ffangg didn't accept the challenge, she and her brothers would abandon him again, and Ffangg and I both knew it.

"So you and your belly seek to best me in a deadly duel," he said. "Two against one? So be it. Name your day, and I will meet you on the battlefield." He paused. "I mean, in the **Box**."

"I will return in two days," I declared. Then I turned to the kittens. "And when you resume your training with me, don't expect me to treat you so kindly as before!"

"Please do use these next days to prepare yourself,

Wyss-Kuzz. If I am going to go to the trouble of fighting, I would rather it take more than five hectoseconds to rip you to blubbery shreds."

"You will eat your words!" I vowed.

"Well, it certainly seems that you know a lot about *eating*."

His purr echoed in my ears as I left.

Revenge! *You will be mine.*

CHAPTER 49

Tonight was the night that the big-shot Hollywood producers were taking Cam's family out to dinner—which also meant that it was the night for me to make things right again.

I walked past Cameron's house three times, attempting to look cool as I tried to figure out if anyone was home. But I was *not* cool—I was freaked out! I must've walked around the block another four times before I got up the nerve to look in the tiny side window of the garage.

No car. The Addamses had to be gone.

I tiptoed around to the back of the house to the sunporch door. As quietly as I could, I turned the handle. It was locked. So were the windows.

What was I supposed to do now? I was about to give

up and go back home when I saw the old dog door. It was small and super dirty—but it also led right into the sunporch. I got down on my hands and knees and poked my head through the greasy plastic flap. Next I wedged my shoulders through, which wasn't easy. It must have taken another ten minutes for me to squirm the rest of the way inside.

When I stood up, though, there was Dr. Drone, sitting in the same place as before, almost like it was waiting for me. I breathed a sigh of relief. This was going to be easier than I'd thought! No one would ever know how close I had come to humiliating my former best friend.

I opened the hood of the robot where the recorder was and scrolled through the menu to find the hidden track. There were two options—ERASE and RECORD. I was just about to press the first one when *Cameron* walked in.

I immediately froze. "What are you doing here?" I yelped.

"What am *I* doing here?" he said. "I live here!"

"But you were supposed to be out at that movie dinner thing!" I said.

"My stupid parents made me stay home because it's a school night. The real question is what are *you* doing in the Americaman room?"

"I came here to—uh—leave you a card. To say sorry about the other day. You know, like, an apology?"

Cameron's eyes narrowed to slits.

"Where's the card, then?"

"Um, that's the funny thing," I said. "I forgot it!"

"You think I'm an idiot?" he said, his voice furious. "And blind? You're trying to sabotage Dr. Drone!"

"No, Cam, I'm not. I—"

"You're trying to get revenge, is that it?" he said. "Because you think I messed with your dumb water robot! Well, the joke's on you, because I didn't!"

"I know! That's why I'm trying to—"

"But I *wish* I had!" Cameron said. "The look on your faces! You and your stupid friends—it was priceless. Where did you find those losers?"

Cam burst into laughter, and I remembered all over again how he talked behind my back. I *hate* it when people talk behind someone else's back.

I pressed RECORD.

"What are the names of those two?" Cameron said. "Pinecone and Stevia? They are totally pitiful! But everyone at this school is a loser. At least, compared to all the kids back in Brooklyn. I mean, how pathetic are those guys Max and Brody? They're so boring, I can't even tell them apart, except that one of them has those dumb glasses. And those two kids on my robotics team! Newt's not so bad, except she's so in love with me, it's scary. And Scorpion—he's the worst kid in this entire pathetic excuse for a city! That dude has got the brains of a lobotomized flea!"

As Cam started laughing again, I touched STOP and closed the hood of Dr. Drone.

"Well, you caught me," I said, getting up to go. "I guess I'm going to just have to watch you win yet again with your awesome robot."

"Yes, you will!" Cam said. "And go out the way you

came in—through the *dog* door."

As I wiggled my way through, any worries that maybe I'd done something I shouldn't have went right out of my mind.

CHAPTER 50

My training regimen was far more intense than anything I had assigned the kitten commandos. I had established a strenuous obstacle course down in the bunker, which I raced through repeatedly, besting my time with each subsequent loop. The progression was as follows:

1. Shred one ball of twine and two boxes in quick succession

2. Standing leap to windowsill, midair reversal to soft landing on armchair (or Human, if available)

3. Jump to target, turn, flip, claw-slash

4. Defensive Crouch, side-skitter, vertical leap over laundry basket

5. Wall-run, stair-climb, somersault, roll landing

6. Evil *hissssssssssssssssssss!* for ten seconds

7. Repeat

My diet was similarly extreme. I consumed only milk—my power drink—and raw eggs, which, while disgusting, were revitalizing. My coat shone and shimmered as never before! Except, of course, for my tail.

But even that situation was improved, as the boy-Human had wrapped it in a kind of bandage that the ogres use to give support to injured limbs.

I allowed him to do this so that the bald ugliness of my tail would cease to distract me. However, the wrap had an unexpected benefit: It had turned my tail into a mighty club! As rule 489 of *Better Guerrilla Warfare Through Mind Games* states: *Turn your deficiency into a strength.* With a swish this way or that, my tail could wreak mighty havoc! I went into the kitchen and broke drinking vessel after drinking vessel. It was brilliant!

When the boy-ogre returned home from his school, he looked around in dismay. "What have you done, Klawde? You've destroyed the house! When Mom sees this, she's going to freak!"

Crouch. Swish. Attack!

"Ow!" he said, pushing me off his face. "What's *wrong* with you?"

"I am taking your advice, which, as we all know, was *my* advice to begin with," I declared. "I am preparing for vengeance. You will assist me by being my target!"

"I don't see why I should help you when *you* were the one who sabotaged the Aqua-Bot!"

My ears flattened: Dim-witted though he was, he had uncovered the truth! "Nonsense," I said. "I didn't touch your weapon."

As the saying goes: *An excellent lie is better than an inconvenient truth.*

"And, even if I did do it," I said, "did *you* not tamper

with this other ogre's robot also?"

"But you and I aren't enemies!" he said. "We're FRIENDS!"

I scoffed. "How many times do I have to tell you, I don't know what *friends* means!"

The ogre sighed and began cleaning up the impressive damage I had done. "Why did you even do this?" he said.

I explained to him how I had challenged Ffangg to the Bout of the Box. A fight to the death! He looked horrified.

"Klawde, I don't want you fighting that other space kitty."

I growled low in my throat. "Soon there will be no *other* space kitty."

CHAPTER 51

The Wormy Apple Harvest Festival was Elba Middle School's biggest celebration of the year. Every inch of the school grounds was covered with food carts, produce displays, carnival games, and wormy apple stands. A "wormy apple" was an apple on a stick dipped in brown caramel with a gummy worm sticking out of it. It looked seriously disgusting.

Steve, of course, had eaten six of them, as well as three cones of cotton candy, and he was currently watching the Tuba Club get ready to play the school anthem while eating a giant bag of jelly beans.

"I didn't know we were here to celebrate the *candy* harvest," Cedar said to him. "What kind of plant do jelly beans grow on?"

"Jelly-beanstalks, *duh*," Steve said.

They might have been having fun, but I couldn't enjoy myself one bit. I was way too nervous. I had never done anything this mean before.

"Stop worrying so much," Cedar said. "You did awesome."

I'd told them about going to Cameron's house, and how I was having second thoughts about what I'd done. I wasn't worried about Cam getting into trouble—I might even enjoy that a little—but I *was* worried about **me** getting into trouble. And what about all the kids hearing the nasty things he'd said about them?

Cedar shrugged. "I don't really mind the name Pinecone," she said.

"Yeah, but Stevia's a *girl's* name," Steve said.

"It's actually a plant," Cedar said. "It's used as a healthy alternative to sugar."

Steve's mouth opened in horror. "But sugar is the *best thing in the world.*"

While Cedar and Steve argued over health food versus junk food, I thought about who else I was worried about: Klawde. Could he *really* be having a fight to the death with this Ffangg? I assumed he was exaggerating, but no matter what kind of fight it was, he needed more time. He really didn't look like he was in combat shape.

Steve elbowed me in the ribs. "Here we go," he said, rubbing his hands together. "This is gonna be so good!"

Principal Brownepoint's voice crackled over the loudspeaker. "Turn your eyes to the skies, ladies and gentlemen, and behold the pride of Elba Middle School's robotics class!"

Everyone around us looked up eagerly. First I heard the low buzzing of propellers, and then I saw it: the drone flying low over the booths. It turned and banked, dropping a packet of Band-Aids on the ground in front of the first-aid tent. Then the siren started wailing.

Everyone gasped—it sounded so *real*—and they

began to clap as red and white lights flashed on the drone.

"Why is it still playing the siren?" Steve asked.

I checked the time on my phone.

11:59.

I took a deep breath.

"One more minute," I said.

CHAPTER 52

I felt like a new cat as I journeyed to the citadel of my enemy. From branch to branch I leaped through the trees, my paws never touching ground. I called my enemy forth from a towering oak overhanging Ffangg's yard.

"Come out, coward, wherever you are!" I shouted.

Looking down, I saw that he had prepared the Fight Box, which was his right as the one challenged. He had chosen a particularly small one, perhaps to mock my expanded size.

I didn't care. I would thrash him, no matter what!

"Why do you look to the ground, oh fat one, when you should be looking UP?"

I hissed in surprise. The vile traitor had *also* chosen to approach battle from a high branch.

Everything he knew, he learned from me! I, however,

didn't teach him everything that *I* knew.

"Are you ready, foe?" I asked. "Your next nap will be underground."

Ffangg licked his paw. "It will be *you* who goes to join our ancestors, not I," he said. "Perhaps I shall bury you in that litter box of which you are so fond."

"Enough small talk," I said. "Let us enter the Box."

We jumped down from the trees in which we had been perched and faced off in the grass. The kittens, I now saw, were situated upon the peaked roof of a low shed. Their inquisitive eyes tracked our every move.

"You first," Ffangg said. "Age before power."

"No, no, after *you*," I said. "Treachery before greatness!"

Several subsequent moments were spent in vicious hissing.

I decided to end negotiations by boldly leaping into the Box, but as I prepared to do so, something spectacular happened.

The sky was rent by a **green flash**!

A craft hovered above us, whirring softly. Slowly it descended, landing right next to the Fight Box.

The module opened, and

out of it came . . .

FLOOFFEE-FYR!!

CHAPTER 53

Most of Elba had turned out for the big event, and they all stood there with their mouths open as they watched the drone swoop and dive over our heads. Principal Brownepoint's staticky voice was getting drowned out by Scorpion, who kept cranking up the volume of the siren.

Miss Natasha came hurrying over. "Too loud!" she shouted.

"HEY! WHY IS THE SIREN STILL PLAYING?" Cedar yelled in my ear.

I had no idea—it was 12:02!

It was then that I realized I hadn't checked the clock in Dr. Drone's recorder. Oh no! What if it wasn't set to the right time? Or the right date? For all I knew, the hidden track wouldn't switch over until the year 2525!

But even as I worried, something *nobody* was expecting happened.

A green flash lit up the whole sky.

"OOOOOH!" the crowd went.

"Hey, how'd those guys do THAT?" I heard Max holler.

"Because Cameron is just THAT COOL!" Brody yelled back.

It had to have *something* to do with Klawde, but before I could even begin to think what, the siren stopped and a voice boomed from the sky above us.

Cameron's voice.

" . . . *everyone at this school is a loser. At least, compared to all the kids back in Brooklyn . . .*"

Everyone at the fair was still looking up at the flying, talking drone. And now it seemed like they were all holding their breath.

"*. . . I mean, how pathetic are those guys Max and Brody? They're so boring, I can't even tell them apart,*

except that one of them has those dumb glasses."

Max looked like he wanted to cry, and I felt terrible.

While the recording played, Cameron ran over to

Scorpion. He yelled, "Gimme that! Gimme that!" and tried to snatch the controls out of his hand. But Scorpion held them over his head.

"I wanna listen," he said.

"Newt's not so bad, except she's so in love with me, it's scary . . ."

"So not!" Newt shouted.

"So are!" Scorpion laughed.

"And Scorpion—he's the worst kid in this entire pathetic excuse for a city! That dude has got the brains of a lobotomized flea!"

Scorpion had stopped laughing.

"It . . . it's not *true*," Cameron said, backing away from him.

Scorpion held out the remote for me to take.

"Hold this, loser," he said.

As Scorpion took off after Cameron, the entire school broke into a cheer.

CHAPTER 54

My prayers and dreams! They had been **answered**! Flooffee-Fyr had returned! Finally!!

"Well, well, well," Ffangg hissed. "Just *look* who came fleeing to Earth."

The miserable lackey exited the module and slunk toward me, his head hung low.

"It's all too much being the Supremest Leader!" Flooffee said. "I can't handle it anymore! It's impossible to rule a planet of **cats**! Nobody listens or follows directions, and no one is loyal to anything or anybody! You were right, oh lord and master! I can't rule Lyttyrboks by myself. You can have the Scepter of Power back. I just want to be your right-paw cat again, oh omnipotent warlord!"

My whiskers tingled with resurgent pride—with

victory! I knew it! I **knew** the day of my triumphant return would come. I turned to my kitten commandos. "Troops!" I cried. "Come with me! Let us return to Lyttyrboks, where you shall taste the sweet nectar of conquest!"

The calico's eyes flashed with malice and delight. Her brothers looked eager to follow my lead.

"Do you hear that, Ffangg?" I said, whirling back around. "Flooffee has come back so he can serve me! Not you—ME! Ffangg! *Ffangg?*"

I scanned the yard for my rival. When I saw what was happening, my jaw dropped in horror.

Ffangg was climbing into the module!

"It would seem that there is a sudden opening for Supreme Leader back home," Ffangg called. "A position most naturally filled by **me**."

I lunged for the module, but Ffangg pulled up on the hover controls, and my claws scratched empty air.

"You have lost, Wyss-Kuzz! Give it up!" Ffangg snarled. "You are an Earth cat now, and an Earth cat you shall remain. You are . . . *KLAWDE*."

But all of a sudden, the calico lunged from the roof of the shed and landed right on the space module! Her two brothers quickly followed her. They would be my salvation! They would overpower Ffangg and return the module to me! They would climb inside . . .

. . . and close the hatch behind them.

A burst of green light blinded me.

They were gone.

Gone gone.

I turned to Flooffee.

"Are you . . . telling me . . . that you left the wormhole protocols *open*?" I said. "And the keys in the ignition of the module?"

"Well, I . . . uh . . . thought we were going right back to Lyttyrboks," Flooffee said. "Like, um, to reconquer it with you in charge and all?"

"But that's *not* going to happen now, is it?" I said.

"Uh, I guess not."

"Because now *Ffangg* is going to conquer it. With *my* commandos!"

Flooffee shrank smaller at my words. "Um, yeah, it's kinda looking that way," he whimpered. "But, uh, one thing, oh master?"

"What is it, you sniveling fool?"

"What happened to your tail?"

My blood boiled like a thousand volcanoes. "You witless, cross-eyed hairball with legs! I shall skin you alive!"

I pounced, but Flooffee had already darted away. He always *was* quicker than he looked! But when I caught that fluffy moron, I would make him pay. Oh, would I make him **pay**!

CHAPTER 55

Principal Brownepoint made Cam take a seminar on verbal bullying after the Harvest Festival disaster. Cam also had to write long letters of apology to Cedar, Steve, Max, Brody, Newt, Scorpion, and . . . **me**.

He delivered it on a Saturday morning, along with a bag of everything bagels, just like we used to eat back in Brooklyn.

"Thanks," I said, feeling sort of awkward about the whole situation. "But why did you write *me* a letter? You didn't even insult me on the recording."

"I know," he said. "But I was mean to you—not just here in Elba, but also back in Brooklyn. I should have taken you to Comic-Con instead of Bronco Jones."

"It's okay," I said. "I mean, Bronco *is* really cool."

Cam shrugged. "You know, I used to think *you* were

the cool kid and *I* was the dork. Remember? When all those kids started wanting to hang out with me, it was awesome. But it was all because of my mom."

Suddenly, I felt like a total jerk for what I had done. "I'm sorry I recorded you," I said.

"I'm sorry for what I said about your friends."

I smiled. "Scorpion sort of deserved it, though."

Cam smiled, and it kind of seemed like we might be friends again.

Someday.

When I got home, I was feeling pretty good about the way things had ended with Cam. But Klawde was *not*.

"I have never been more disgusted by you," he snarled. "You and your Human notions of 'apology' and 'forgiveness.' You make me want to cough up a thousand hairballs."

If Klawde sounded a little grumpier than usual, it was with good reason. Ffangg had had more success reconquering Lyttyrboks than he could have ever imagined, and Klawde was torturing himself by following every minute of the conquest on some kind of intergalactic feline news messaging app.

"Klawde, maybe you should just turn that off and—I don't know—go torment Flabby Tabby a little?"

He hissed at me.

What upset him the most was that the *true* source of Ffangg's power was Klawde's own kitten commandos. They had proved themselves to be just as ferocious a fighting force as he'd hoped they'd be.

It was a few days later that I heard a strange noise coming from the basement—a noise like I'd never heard from Klawde before. It sounded like a hyena on helium.

I hurried downstairs. "Are you okay, Klawde?"

"Okay? *Okay?*" Klawde shouted. "I am better than okay! Oh, joyous day! The sensible felines of Lyttyrboks have overthrown that miserable, traitorous wretch! They are free of his tyranny, which means that they are ready for *my* tyranny! I must prepare. Surely this means that the Council will send for me. I—I—"

He was distracted by a new story flashing onto his Intra-Universal Feline News Feed. And immediately, his cackle turned to a gasp of horror.

Unfortunately for Klawde, it turned out that it wasn't the entire feline population of Lyttyrboks who had overthrown Ffangg. It was, instead, one *particular* feline. And she wasn't even from Lyttyrboks.

She was from Earth.

ABOUT THE AUTHORS

Although a worthless Human, **Johnny Marciano** has redeemed himself somewhat by chronicling the glorious adventures of Klawde, Evil Alien Warlord Cat. His lesser work concerns the pointless doings of other worthless Humans, in books such as *The Witches of Benevento*, *The No-Good Nine*, and *Madeline at the White House*. He currently resides on the planet New Jersey.

Emily Chenoweth is a despicable Human living in Portland, Oregon, where the foul liquid known as rain falls approximately 140 days a year. Under the top secret alias Emily Raymond, she has collaborated with James Patterson on numerous best-selling books. There are three other useless Humans in her family, and two extremely ignorant Earth cats.

For Luke—JM

For everyone at Abernethy Elementary,
especially the student journalists
of the Abernethy Talon—EC

For my parents, Barb and Brad.
Thanks for all the stories, drawings,
and unending support—RM

W

PENGUIN WORKSHOP
An Imprint of Penguin Random House LLC, New York

Text copyright © 2019 by John Bemelmans Marciano and Emily Chenoweth. Illustrations copyright © 2019 by Robb Mommaerts. All rights reserved. First published in hardcover in 2019 by Penguin Workshop. This paperback edition published in 2020 by Penguin Workshop, an imprint of Penguin Random House LLC, New York. PENGUIN and PENGUIN WORKSHOP are trademarks of Penguin Books Ltd, and the W colophon is a registered trademark of Penguin Random House LLC. Manufactured in China.

Visit us online at www.penguinrandomhouse.com.

Library of Congress Control Number: 2018061169

ISBN 9780593225240   10 9 8 7 6 5 4 3 2 1